And the Winner Is

HOLLYWOOD REBELS AND ROMEOS
BOOK FIVE

OLIVIA JAYMES

And the Winner Is

Sierra Oliver's flirting skills are virtually non-existent. Married young to her high school boyfriend, she hasn't had much experience with men. Now single, she's vowed to have some fun and do all of the things she's missed. Falling in love and getting serious are not on the agenda. Casual relationships only.

When she meets a handsome and charming man in a bookstore, it's nothing more than a pleasant encounter. She never expected to see or speak to him again, so it's a surprise to find out that he's the director of her new movie. Ryan Ward has a well-earned reputation as a ladies' man, dating one beautiful actress after another. She'd do well to stay far away from him.

But the air crackles with electricity whenever Sierra and Ryan are in the same room. Her sister is encouraging her to go for it. Have a fun fling and then move on. No looking back. No hard feelings. Sierra is tempted, but she has a feeling that Ryan is completely out of her league. A man like that is a sexy motorcycle while she's still in training wheels...

Does she dare take a chance on the hottest director in Hollywood?

CHAPTER

One

SIERRA OLIVER DUCKED into the bookstore and shook out her wet hair, the tendrils already curling from the humidity. It was raining cats and dogs and guinea pigs out there, and the cold wind was nasty as well. They were lucky it was only a rainstorm. In the Midwest in the middle of March it just as easily could have been a blizzard.

The four walls of her temporary lodging had felt like they were closing in on her and she simply couldn't stay inside any longer. That's how she'd found herself battling the elements and walking to the bookstore. First stop was the little cafe that took up the corner of the shop. The whole store smelled of delicious coffee and chocolate and her stomach growled in protest, reminding her that she hadn't yet eaten dinner. Her desire to get out of the same four walls had been greater than her hunger. The food smelled delicious, but she managed to talk herself out of the yummy pastry and only ordered a latte before heading to her favorite section.

She didn't need any more books. Not really, but one or two more wouldn't hurt. Buying books wasn't the worst habit in the world. Pulling one from the large selection, Sierra flipped through the hardbound book and then placed it back onto the shelf. It wasn't quite what she was looking for.

Strolling the aisles of the local bookstore on a stormy Friday night wasn't the most exciting activity but it was more than fine as far as she was concerned. It was quiet here, just a few patrons browsing while others sat in the cafe section reading or chatting. A few tapped away at their laptops, ignoring everyone around them.

She'd pick up a book or two then stop by that funky restaurant on the corner and order some takeout. While the rest of the cast was out drinking and partying, enjoying their time off, she was happy to putter around the downtown area of the small town she'd inhabited for the last six weeks making a movie.

A movie that had come to an abrupt halt three days ago when the director crumpled to the floor with a heart attack right on the set. He'd been taken away in an ambulance and word was that he wouldn't be returning. The studio was dispatching a replacement as soon as possible to finish the filming but until then she was at loose ends. She'd spent the last few days happily ensconced in a comfortable chair by her front window reading a book and sipping hot chocolate but she was anxious to get back to work and finish.

She loved to read and if she had her way she'd buy a stack of books she didn't need. Already, she had a to-be-read pile in the dozens weighing down her luggage when she traveled. There was always downtime between scenes and picking up a good book was an excellent way to pass the time and keep the boredom at bay. She really needed to pick up one of those e-readers so that she didn't have to drag paperbacks around the globe.

Now this one looks interesting.

The cover was dark and hinted at a delightfully grue-some murder between the pages. She liked mysteries the best. After working through all of Agatha Christie's novels as a teenager she'd been well and truly hooked on the genre. She loved it when an amateur sleuth solved the murder in the last chapter. It was even better when she figured it out before the main character.

Another cover caught her eye, an author she'd read before and liked. Moving her coffee to her other hand and hitching her handbag higher on her shoulder, she reached for the title but at the same time another hand reached for it as well. Both of them jerked their arms back quickly when their fingers lightly brushed. The skin was warm despite the chilly temperatures just outside.

I just touched a stranger.

Clutching her coffee to her chest, she took a deep breath, looking up to see the person who had the same taste in books that she did.

A male. Handsome, too. If you liked the rugged type. Dark hair that looked slightly windswept from the rain-storm outside. Tanned skin that was definitely out of place in the middle of winter. Was he naturally like that or had he been to some warm and exotic locale recently?

White teeth and dimples. She could tell because he was smiling. It wouldn't hurt to smile back, would it? Being friendly was a good thing.

"Sorry about that," the man said, waving a hand toward the shelf. "You can have it."

Maybe that smile hadn't been such a great idea. She hadn't thought he would speak to her. Was he flirting? She felt a moment of panic as she studied his face more closely, looking for a clue. She didn't know and she didn't have the experience to figure it out. Flirting was something she'd never learned, not that she wanted to do it with him. But it was a female skill she'd missed out on. Like so many other things.

Just be nice and friendly. It's no big deal. People talk to each other all the time.

"No, you take it. I think I'm going to look at this one instead."

"There's more than one copy if we both want it." He moved a step closer and that's when she noticed how tall he was. At least six foot and maybe more. At five-seven she wasn't exactly short but he made her feel tiny.

That internal warning voice was talking in her ear. Telling her that she didn't know anything about this guy and he could be a real asshole.

Sierra took two steps backward, putting space between them. He was a stranger and although he seemed perfectly harmless, he could be a crazy serial killer for all she knew. She had terrible judgment about people. Especially men.

She had a bad habit of thinking the best of someone when they were actually a horrible human being.

"Thank you," she replied politely. "But I'm going to pass on that one."

She didn't want to be rude. Turning back to the shelves, she perused the titles, hopefully letting the gentleman know she wasn't interested in starting a conversation.

He didn't get the hint, however. If he did, he was ignoring it.

Instead he also began to study the bookshelves, his body parallel to hers. "I don't suppose you could recommend one of these? I'm not much of a mystery fan but I kind of need to study one."

He looked too old to be a student but this was a college town in the Midwest, so it was possible. He held up the book they'd both been interested in.

"What about this one? Is this a good author?"

It wouldn't hurt to talk to him. Give advice. No one ever asked for her opinion so this was something new. She didn't have any education after high school, so most people simply assumed she didn't know much. In fact, she didn't think she was all that smart but she did know her mystery novels.

"It is." Sierra nodded, her cheeks warm with embarrassment. She didn't know why she was embarrassed to talk about her favorite authors and books but she was. She'd tried to read the literary novels, the classics, but she liked these better. It was more fun to work out the puzzle. "I haven't read that particular novel but the author is excellent. She knows how to keep you guessing the whole way through. Lots of twists and turns."

"That's exactly what I need." He paged through the book and then turned to the back. "Do you ever cheat and read the ending first?"

Eyes wide, Sierra shook her head, slightly scandalized by the mere suggestion. "No! That would ruin all the fun. You can't do that."

She had an urge to reach over and slam his book shut so he couldn't read the ending but she didn't give in to it. It wasn't really her business but it seemed so wrong.

"No one would know."

"I'd know." She wasn't the rebel type but he clearly was. "Do you do that a lot?"

"Do what?"

"Break the rules."

This time he did laugh, his blue eyes twinkling with mirth. "I don't think there's a rule about reading the end of a mystery first."

Maybe, but...

"It's an unwritten rule," she argued. "Everyone knows you're not supposed to do that. Why read the book if you already know the ending?"

He seemed to consider her question, rubbing his chin in thought. "Have you ever seen a movie based on a book?"

"Yes."

He grinned as if she'd admitted to stealing the family silver. "But you already knew the ending."

From the smirk on his face, he thought he was so clever.

"It's not the same. When you see a movie based on a novel, you're going to see the filmmaker's adaptation of the story. His or her vision. When you read a book, you're still in the discovery stage. It's different."

"You've given this a lot of thought."

Not really. Or maybe she had. Either way it only seemed logical. But she had sort of climbed up on a soapbox and there was no real reason he should care about her opinions.

"I apologize. I don't mean to go on about it."

"It's fine. It's actually quite refreshing to see someone that's so passionate about stories."

The director hadn't thought so. He'd basically told her she was pretty scenery and she needed to shut up and just do her job. She wasn't paid to have ideas or suggestions.

He held up the book. "So I should get this? Maybe we both should."

The author was excellent... Sierra plucked the book from the shelf.

"I don't think you'll be disappointed."

"I appreciate your help."

They'd run out of conversation and the moment had become slightly awkward. She didn't want him to think she was interested or that she was the type of woman that could be picked up in the mystery section of a bookstore.

"Well, have a nice evening. Hope you enjoy the book."

"You too."

For a moment she thought he might say something else but then he turned and waved as he headed to the front of the store and the cashier. She watched him out of the corner of her eye as he paid for his book, all while pretending that she was studying a stack of books on a table.

He really was quite handsome. Not that she cared.

She wasn't looking for a man. Not one special man, anyway. She was looking for...life. Or better yet...experiences. She'd missed out on so much. She wanted to travel and date and flirt and eat strange food. She wanted to drive too fast and stay up all night without worrying about getting up for work the next morning. She wanted to learn to play guitar and dance like no one was watching. There were so many things Sierra hadn't done because she was too busy simply surviving.

She wanted to make up for lost time.

———

I should have asked her for coffee or something.

Ryan Ward wasn't a man that came on to strange but lovely women in bookstores. He simply wasn't the type. For the last several years the women had come to him. It wasn't vanity or ego, either. A successful movie director that didn't have two noses and three eyes was in demand with the female species. They all wanted to be stars and they thought the road to fame and fortune led straight through his bedroom. Those ladies were destined to be disappointed. He wasn't the kind of guy that slept with women and then gave them movie roles. The two activities were kept separate in his life.

He'd taken one look at the woman in the bookstore and become instantly smitten. He'd seen women more beautiful but there had been something about her that captured his attention and held it. Maybe it was the way she'd pinched her brows together when she'd read the back of the spine or how she'd smiled when she'd found a book she'd liked and then tucked it under her arm so protectively. Or perhaps it was the keen interest and intelligence he'd seen in the depths of those gold and green eyes. She was more than just a pretty face, and the rest of her wasn't anything to sneeze at either.

Slim but with some curves. She was wearing a tight pair of blue jeans that hugged those long legs and cute little bottom. It was hard to tell how long her hair was since she was wearing a thick coat with a hood, but it was at least shoulder length with a mix of brown and gold running through it. Her skin was creamy with just a touch of pink on the cheeks from the cold without a trace of makeup. So different from the women he usually spent time around.

Which automatically made her fascinating. That's why he'd almost gone out of his comfort zone and asked to buy her a coffee. And he didn't even know her name.

Too late. Your chance has passed.

With a sigh, he picked up the bag containing the mystery novel she'd recommended and headed back out into the rain, sheltering his purchase under his jacket as he hurried down the sidewalk. He'd go back to the condo he was staying in temporarily, fix a bite to eat, pour a glass of wine, and then get ready for work in the morning. He was here to do a job, not meet pretty girls. It wouldn't be a good idea anyway to get involved with a local. It wasn't a good idea to get involved with anyone. Period. His career was finally going the way he wanted it to and he wasn't going to be sidetracked by love. He'd seen enough movies to know that love could make a man behave like an idiot.

I don't need any help acting stupid. I've got that covered.

Besides, picking up a girl in a bookstore was too cliché. Too romantic comedy. Too Tom Hanks and Meg Ryan.

He certainly wasn't going to find Ms. Right in the local bookstore. Frankly, if he hadn't found her yet, he doubted she really existed.

CHAPTER
Two

"I HEARD the new director is Ryan Ward. He's a notorious hard ass. I heard he's made grown men cry."

That declaration was made by Tony Gillette over coffee the next morning as Sierra and the rest of the cast gathered to meet the new director who was going to finish the film. She'd received the message last night that she needed to be on set by eight. It would be good to get back to work.

Tony was playing the lead actor's best friend and the person he was talking to was Angela Brenner, the lead actress. The fact that Tony knew and Angela didn't surprised Sierra. If anyone should know about a replacement first it should have been the leads. Of which Sierra was not one. In this romantic comedy, she was playing one of Angela's friends. It was a small but rather juicy role as she had some smart and funny lines. She'd been fortunate to get the part. The former director had reminded her of this fact almost daily.

"That's good news. Are you sure?" Angela asked, filling her plate from the craft services table. Absolutely no carbs. It was all protein, all the time for the leading lady. Sierra often felt like she had to hide in the bathroom when she ate a piece of bread. She'd get dirty looks from the cast and crew. "I wouldn't mind working for him. He's won an Oscar, you know."

Ryan Ward? Sierra knew that name. He'd directed a film last year that had snagged several awards. A modern day take on *Macbeth*. She'd never read the play but she'd watched the movie twice. It had been that good. She'd also heard that he was dating the leading lady. She'd been nominated for Best Actress.

Tony rolled his eyes and snorted. "I don't think his mere presence on this film is going to get any of us an award. This isn't his usual highbrow stuff. Someone must have called in a favor to get him to do it."

Angela didn't get a chance to reply. The assistant director Burt was waving his arms and calling to all of them to gather on the soundstage. It looked like it was time to meet their new director.

Sierra squeezed in next to the makeup artist, sort of off to the side of the large group but near the front so she could see. There were several people milling around and she recognized a few of them as the producers of the movie. She'd met them when she'd signed the contract for the role. A tall man had his back to the crowd, and she assumed that it must be their new director.

He was tall. Dressed in faded blue jeans and a t-shirt, he had wide shoulders and powerful arms. Not to mention a really nice rear view. Apparently, Ryan Ward spent some of his free time working out when he wasn't making movies and romancing beautiful and famous actresses.

She took a bite of her lemon poppy seed muffin and choked slightly when he turned around to face the group. She easily recognized the crooked grin, the dark brown hair that was now dry, and the intense stare that seemed to take in everything around him.

It was the handsome mystery reader from the bookstore last night.

And he'd aimed his blue gaze directly at her.

———

Ryan had never thought to see the pretty woman from the bookstore again but here she was and apparently, she worked on this film. In what capacity he wasn't sure but this was surely a sign from fate. He meant to talk to her again, and he would, just as soon as he was done addressing the cast and crew.

"Thank you for the warm welcome," he said after being introduced by the producer. The crowd applauded and his face went warm. He wasn't used to that shit. He was a director, not an actor. He worked behind the scenes and that was fine. He had no desire to put his life in the spotlight. "I'm really happy to be here, although these are sad circumstances. I want you to know that I spoke with Stan just this morning and he's doing much better. He'll be recovering at home in Beverly Hills and he wishes us well. We spoke at length about his vision for this movie and my job here is to continue that journey. I may have a signature brand but this isn't about me. I'm here to finish Stan's film, not make my own mark. He's been a good friend through the years and this is my way of giving back. So I don't think there will be many changes going forward. Of course, Stan and I do work differently but we'll all get used to this together. If you have any questions or concerns, please don't hesitate to speak with me. I'm on a first name basis with all the cast and crew on my pictures and I don't want it to be any different here."

Yes, I definitely want to know that beauty's name.

"I'll be having one on one meetings with the senior crew and also the actors. I want to get a feel for what you think is going well and what could be improved. For the actors I want to discuss your characters and their arcs. We'll be setting those up right away. As for today, I'm planning to have those meetings in between shooting some background sets. Tomorrow we'll be up and running. Any questions?"

No one said anything but Ryan didn't expect them to. He'd hit them with a lot of information, plus they were all probably surprised that he was here. This wasn't his usual type of film and they had to all be wondering what made him sign on. It literally was because of his friendship with Stan but Hollywood was so cynical no one was going to believe that.

He'd first speak with the crew, and then he'd start in on the cast. He immediately recognized Angela, who was playing the female lead. He'd heard a few things about her and hardly any of it was good. She made trouble on the set, acted like a diva, and slept with all of her co-stars and a few of the extras for good measure. Since her male lead Henry Goodwin was a happily married man Ryan wasn't sure who she was going to try her wiles out on. He sure as hell wasn't interested.

"Thank you all. Everyone is being given a call sheet with your assignments. Let's all work together and get this movie done for Stan."

More applause but this time it sounded truly genuine. Stan was a nice guy and a good director, although he was a *man's* director. He didn't do women and their feelings all that well, and he didn't enjoy it, either. Stan wanted to do car crashes and gunfire fights. That was what was so interesting about him taking this romantic comedy. It was probably a deal with the studio. *Do this film and we'll let you do this other one.*

Gary, the producer, handed Ryan a stack of file folders as the crowd dispersed. "Here are your main actors. Their head shots and resumes are in there. I think you'll be happy with all of them. The dailies that we've been seeing from Stan were excellent."

In better circumstances, Ryan would have made sure to see the footage already shot but he'd been in Milan when he'd received the frantic call to step in. Wrapping up the location scouting he'd been doing for his next film, he'd then packed his bag and flown here. Exhausted but ready to work. Tonight he'd watch all the footage. At least twice.

"Thanks, Gary. I'll look through them."

"We really appreciate you stepping in, Ryan. You're saving our asses here."

"I'm happy to help Stan."

Ryan didn't really trust Gary Thomson all that much.

He had a slimy reputation as a ladies man who liked to party. As for whether the women were always willing, that was up for debate. The casting couch was alive and well in show business, although it was becoming more and more of an anachronism. But some men held on to the past longer than others. If the rumors were true, Gary was one of them. Ryan, however, tried not to judge people based on gossip. He'd never worked with the producer before so as far as he was concerned, innocent until he saw something different.

I'll be keeping my eyes open.

Thomson scurried away and Ryan paged through the files, stopping when he opened one and saw her face again.

Sierra Oliver.

She wasn't all that seasoned of an actress. She'd made a few films but her resume was thin. She was extremely attractive with long dark hair and big green eyes. She was playing the role of the best friend, which in Ryan's opinion was the juiciest role in the movie. Well-written and funny, the part was ripe for stealing the picture.

If the right actress were cast. Was Sierra the right person? She didn't have much experience and nothing she'd done so far had been comedic. People always thought dramas were the hardest thing to play but it was really comedy. An actor had to have the right timing. It was instinctual and innate. Ryan had worked with actors in the past to try and help them learn but it didn't appear to be a skill like juggling. The more they practiced they didn't necessarily get any better.

He had an appointment with the assistant director and

then he was going to meet with each of the actors and discuss their roles. There were only a few weeks left of principal photography but he had time to fix any issues that there might be. But he needed to know about them first.

The first person he was going to meet with? Sierra.

CHAPTER
Three

THE MORNING WENT RATHER QUICKLY for Sierra. She had a costume fitting and then the hairdresser wanted to try a new style for an upcoming scene. By the time her meeting with Ryan Ward rolled around she was starving, but lunch was going to have to wait.

Excited. Anxious. Ready to jump out of her skin.

She felt all those things and more, in turns dreading and then anticipating the meeting. There had been a spark of attraction - at least on her side - last night. Not that she intended to act on it. Ryan Ward was the director. A romance between them was out of the question.

She wasn't looking for love right now anyway. If she dated, there would be no strings. If she slept with some-one, it would be casual. Love and commitment were not in her near future. That was something for later. Much later. If ever.

The door of his trailer swung open immediately after she knocked as if he was waiting for her. He probably was anxious to get these meetings over with. He had a mountain of work ahead of him to get caught up with all that Stan had done, plus the schedule of scenes that still needed to be shot. Some of them were absolutely vital to the story.

"Come on in, Sierra. You're right on time."

Was that unusual? Did people just randomly show up whenever they wanted to? He was used to working with big stars - like her brother-in-law Tyler Gaylord - but she didn't think Tyler would do that. He'd given her a lecture about work ethic and professionalism when she'd accepted her first role. It was advice she'd taken seriously.

Not sure what to say or do, Sierra stood by the door to the trailer. It was strange to see him again. She'd been so sure she never would but here he was. In the flesh. All six-plus feet of him. And he was her director. They'd be spending a great deal of time together for the next two to three weeks.

Motioning to a seat at a small table, Ryan took the chair opposite. Their knees brushed underneath and a zing of electricity rang up her leg. He was far too attractive today. He'd looked good wet last night but now she could see that his dark hair was a little wavy. He could use a haircut and a shave. His jaw was decorated with stubble that only seemed to emphasize how strong and square it was. He could have been a leading man if he'd wanted to be. "I took the liberty of ordering us some lunch. Craft services seemed to know your preferences. I thought we could eat and chat. Get to know one another."

"Thank you." Her voice was finally working and words were actually being formed. "That sounds like a good idea. I'm ravenous."

He had indeed ordered lunch and it was her favorite. A grilled chicken sandwich with some secret recipe of spices that the chef wouldn't divulge along with steamed broccoli that actually tasted amazing. She'd never liked green vegetables much but this was delicious.

Twisting the cap off a bottle of water, he handed it to her before opening one for himself.

"So why don't you start telling me about yourself. Your background and how you got into acting."

Sierra didn't like talking about herself. Her life story wasn't pretty and she never wanted to sound like she expected sympathy. She wasn't a victim. She'd taken control of her life with a hell of a lot of help from her sister Billie and Billie's husband Tyler. If not for them she might still be waiting tables at that crappy diner in Wisconsin and dodging her husband's fists at night.

"I grew up in the Midwest. Wisconsin. I have a twin sister. You may have heard of her. Billie Oliver Gaylord. That's how I became interested in the movie business. I worked as an assistant to Billie on her film with Sam Collins before being cast in my first role."

Brief. To the point. Everyone thought that Sierra was cast because of her connections so she might as well get them right out there so they could move past it.

Ryan smiled and took a swig of his water. "I've never had the pleasure of meeting your sister but I did meet Tyler at a charity function a few years ago. Great guy and solid actor. I'm looking forward to seeing the film your sister made with Sam. The trailer looks amazing."

That was one of the surprises to Sierra when she'd joined her sister in Hollywood. It took forever and a day to get a movie released. Filming was only one small part of the process. Between editing, reshoots, marketing, and distribution it might be over a year before a movie was released to the public.

"They're very proud of the final product. I haven't seen the final cut but what I did see was terrific. I think you'll enjoy it."

She took another bite of her sandwich which was mouthwatering, but her stomach was tumbling in her abdomen under the weight of Ryan Ward's scrutiny. His gaze was intent, rarely wavering from her face. As a director, he probably did study faces and expressions but it felt unnerving to be...examined like this. It took all her effort not to squirm in her chair. She didn't want him to know that he affected her in any way.

"So, Sierra...how do you feel about your role? Are you satisfied with the screen time that your character gets?"

That question was a trap. Some actors were obsessed with screen minutes and number of lines in a script. They couldn't ever get enough and were constantly pushing for more, even at the expense of others in the production. He was testing her and she didn't like it.

"I think Molly makes an impact in the scenes she's in."

Ryan flipped open a script that was sitting on the table. "I think Molly is a terrific character. One an actress can really sink her teeth into if she has the ability."

Was he asking if she had that ability? He doubted it? Frankly, so did she. She hadn't been in this industry long enough to believe in herself. To be confident. She didn't think she was bad but she wasn't sure she was good, either.

"I hope I can do her justice. I love the character."

His shrewd gaze took in far too much. "But you're not confident."

"No," she admitted. "I'm not. I've only been in a few movies."

He nodded and stroked his chin. "I know that you're new to the business and that makes it hard to know what you don't know. I think Molly has the potential to steal the picture and launch you into bigger and better roles. Would you be willing to work with me a little bit? We could run lines together, talk about how the scene should unfold. It's fine if you don't want to or have other commitments but I think it would take your performance up a notch. Of course, that's me running off at the mouth when I haven't even seen your work yet. You might be doing it perfectly and I need to just leave it alone."

Billie had given Sierra a different lecture from Tyler's. It was about producers and directors who would try and get into her panties. They'd dangle roles in front of her but they came with a price.

Was Ryan Ward that type? She hadn't heard anything like that about him and Hollywood was a small corporate town. There weren't many secrets. He certainly didn't need to use force to get a woman into bed but abusers weren't about sex. They were about power.

But he already gave you an out. You don't have to do it if you don't want to.

Her hesitation must have set off alarm bells because he slapped himself in the forehead and smiled sheepishly. "Jesus, how that must have sounded to you. This is not me coming on strong or making a play, Sierra. This is business only, I swear. I don't have any future roles to promise you and nothing bad will happen if you tell me that you have this all under control. It's all good. I'm just trying to make this picture the best it can be and dammit, I love this character. She's a real pistol and ten times more interesting than either of the leads. If you're worried about me being a lecher we can work at a cafe or coffeehouse. I can understand why you might not feel comfortable being alone with me."

That...didn't sound too bad. In public. With people watching.

She couldn't say yes, though. He might not be attracted to her but she was attracted to him. Chronologically she was an adult but when it came to romance and dating she was really still a teenager. She didn't know the rules. It seemed like a bad idea to place herself in Ryan's company, one on one, when she felt like a schoolgirl around him. Perhaps if she were more sophisticated and worldly she'd do it, but she was a nobody from a piss-ant town in Wisconsin and he was a big-time director who had won an Oscar. She wasn't even remotely in his league.

"I don't think that's a good idea," she finally said when she realized he was still waiting patiently for her answer. "I don't want you to think I don't want to work hard because I do, but I think I'm going to have to pass on your offer. I do want to thank you, though. It's very thoughtful and from what I've seen that's pretty rare in this business."

"I'd like to think it's not that hard to find." He looked disappointed but he didn't press. "I understand your hesitation. We'll work during shooting and just know that I'm here for you if you have any questions or if you change your mind."

He didn't truly get why she turned him down and she had a sneaking suspicion it didn't happen often. She wanted to spread her wings and have some fun. Have some casual sex, maybe. But she needed to start small. Like a little bicycle with training wheels.

Ryan Ward was no kiddie bike. He was a freakin' Harley.

CHAPTER
Four

AFTER A LONG DAY ON SET, all Sierra wanted to do was soak in a hot tub and eat the leftovers in her fridge. An early night sounded like heaven on earth. She was in good shape and had worked hard her whole life but the long hours on set really did take a toll. It was a "hurry up and wait" environment. She was either running around madly or bored out of her mind.

She stripped off her clothes and lowered herself into the steaming water with a sigh of pleasure. Letting the water lap at her chin, she closed her eyes and let all her worries and troubles drift away.

Almost all of them. She was still thinking about Ryan's offer at lunch, and perhaps she'd been shortsighted to turn him down. She wasn't going to jump his bones in public and he certainly wasn't going to put any moves on her in front of God and the little town they were currently in. It would have been completely innocent but she'd said no.

Her nature was to be cautious and watchful. It was

those instincts that had kept her alive all those years with her abusive ex-husband. She'd learned to gauge his moods in mere seconds, although as time went on he hadn't bothered pretending to have a reason to be an asshole.

It was also those instincts that made it difficult to cut loose and take chances. She wanted to do all of the things she'd missed out on but then that voice in her head would start lecturing her about being careful. Luckily, Billie was there to encourage Sierra to follow her dreams whether small, big, silly, or profound. One night in Paris after Billie had finished filming for the day they'd sat in a little cafe, drinking wine and making a list of all the things Sierra wanted to do.

It was a long list. Frankly, some of the items on it were kind of stupid but then they'd had quite a bit of red wine when they'd made it, so it wasn't surprising. She'd been to the top of the Eiffel Tower, she'd had her picture taken at the Hollywood sign on the side of the hill, she'd streaked her hair pink and gone dancing at some crazy nightclub with Tyler and Billie. She'd even gone to a topless beach in the south of France. There was plenty more to do, though. Every time she crossed one off, she added two more.

Hot air ballooning. I should add that.

Her phone chimed a familiar tune, one that told Sierra that her sister was calling to check up on her. Billie and Tyler had been invaluable in getting Sierra back on her feet and they took family seriously.

It just feels good to have my sister again.

Staying in the tub but drying off her hand, Sierra reached for her phone sitting on a stack of towels.

"Hey, sis. What's going on?"

"Tyler heard that Ryan Ward was taking over as director of your movie," Billie said, her voice sounding slightly breathless. "I called as soon as he told me."

"Are you worried about me?"

It wasn't Billie who answered but her movie star husband Tyler Gaylord. "I've never met Ryan Ward but I've heard he can be a real son of a bitch, See. Have you met him yet?"

Twice. I didn't know who he was the first time.

"I did today," she replied instead. "He seems nice, actually. He said he was finishing the picture as a favor to Stan. He also says he's not going to mess with Stan's vision."

Which was a shame. The previous director didn't know much about what made a good chick flick.

"Hmmmm, that's interesting," Tyler said. "Honestly, I wouldn't have pictured either one of them directing a romantic comedy but I'm guessing it was all about contracts and favors. You liked him?"

Very much. Too much.

"I didn't meet with him for that long but he seemed very supportive. He said that he loved the Molly role in the script and thought that it had the potential to steal the picture. He even offered to help me with the role since I'm so new to acting."

There was a silence on the other end of the phone before Sierra's brother-in-law spoke again.

"He offered to help you? That's...unexpected."

Was Tyler thinking that Ryan Ward was a big old horn dog trying to get her into the sack?

"It's not what you're thinking."

"What are we thinking, sis?" Billie asked.

"That he's...you know. He specifically said that we would meet in public, like at a coffeeshop or a cafe. He's not trying to get me into bed."

That seemed to mollify Tyler. "That's good then. I'd hate to have to kill him. I'm glad to know that he'll be helping you. He's a damn good director."

Well...about that...

"I...actually told him no."

More silence. This was becoming an awkward conversation she didn't want to have.

"You told him no," Billie repeated. "Why?"

Because he's too handsome. He makes me nervous.

"He has so many other things to do to get this movie done. I didn't think he'd really have the time."

Lame. Her response was pathetic.

"Don't you think you should let him decide that, See?" Tyler asked, sounding genuinely puzzled about her hesitation to let Ryan Ward coach her in this role. "It can't hurt to meet with him at least once. He might have some insights into playing Molly that you haven't thought about."

Sierra didn't get a chance to respond before Billie interrupted. "Babe, will you run and get that new script that just came in? I want to read part of it to Sierra. I think it's in the office."

"Uh, sure. Yeah. I'll be back in just a minute."

There was the sound of shuffling and then the click of a door.

"Okay, Tyler's gone downstairs and he'll be awhile because that script is sitting right here on the nightstand. Start talking, sis. What's going on there? And don't leave anything out. Was Ryan Ward really a jerk and you didn't want to tell us? Is he the asshole that I've heard about? It wouldn't surprise me."

Sierra sighed, knowing full well that Billie wouldn't leave her alone until she'd spilled her guts of every single detail, no matter how small and insignificant. Resistance was futile.

"No, he really seems nice." She might as well start at the beginning. "I actually sort of met him last night at the bookstore but I didn't know who he was."

"You met him at a bookstore?"

"We both reached for the same book. Then he asked me for a mystery recommendation."

"Really?" Billie sounded intrigued, which was bad. Oh, so bad. There wasn't any intrigue here. "And then what happened?"

"We each paid for our books and left. Separately. I never caught his name and I didn't tell him mine. I didn't think I'd ever see him again and then there he was on the set this morning."

"Did you...want to see him again?"

Sierra didn't lie to Billie. After so many years of being apart and not even speaking to one another they'd made a pact. To always be straight with the truth even if it was difficult. She'd already danced around the crux of it so she might as well get to it.

"Kind of. Maybe. He's...handsome."

"I've seen pictures. He's definitely not ugly. Is that why you turned down his offer of help?"

"Yes," Sierra admitted, relived that Billie saw the situation clearly. "He makes me nervous and uncomfortable."

"Wow," Billie laughed. "Is he that good in person? How does he smell?"

Sierra was about to say that she didn't know but she realized that she did.

"Really good. Like citrus and spice. But not over-whelming like he'd bathed in cologne. Just fresh and clean."

"Oh, that sounds nice," her sister said with a giggle. "So you've been wanting to date and have some fun. What's the problem? He sounds like the perfect guy for you. He's a known womanizer so he won't be getting serious or anything. You can have some fun and then at the end of the shoot just move on."

Billie was way too far ahead. "He never said he wanted to date me. He just asked if he could help me."

"Did he flirt with you in the bookstore?"

"I don't know. I don't have any experience with things like that, remember?"

"Did you flirt with him?"

Had she? She didn't think so.

"No, I don't know how to do that either."

"You do too. I've seen you practice."

And I'm terrible at it. I just can't get the hair flip down pat.

"So you told him no because you want to flirt with him but don't know how?"

Sierra shrugged, although her sister couldn't see her. "I told you he makes me nervous. I do want to date and have some fun but I was thinking that maybe I should start with a man less–"

"Sexy?" Billie broke in, laughing. "Handsome? Masculine?"

"I think he's out of my league. I need to start small. You know, like an aspiring mountain climber doesn't show up at Everest on his first day and try and climb it. He works up to it. Starts with hills, then a small mountain. Then a little bigger. I need to pace myself, sis."

"Ryan Ward as Mount Everest. That's epic. Listen to me, you've been pacing yourself for awhile now but you're just doing laps. You're not getting anywhere. If you really want to mark off a few of those list items you're going to have to take a few chances. What's the worst thing that could happen?"

Humiliation. Shame. Regret. Plague. Pestilence. The four horsemen of the apocalypse.

"I could make a fool of myself."

"You could do that anyway," Billie pointed out. "We all can at any moment. Just let the guy help you. Meet with him. Talk to him like he's an actual human being. If he flirts, flirt back. If he asks you out and you like him, say yes."

She made it sound so easy.

"If we like each other, it could get complicated."

"How complicated could it get in three weeks?" Billie countered. "That's all you have. It's perfect for a little on-set fling. In fact, this is the chance you've been looking for. Sleep with Ryan Ward. No strings, just a casual thing. Let him know the rules. Heck, he's a well-known Lothario so he'll probably be relieved that you aren't looking for marriage and babies. With his reputation I bet he's great in bed."

He didn't have to be great. He only had to be better

than her ex-husband and the bar had been set mighty low right there.

"I'm not sure I can do that."

"Then don't. No one is forcing you to do anything. You're in charge now. You're in command. Not me. Not Tyler. And damn sure not Brian. You. If you want to date, date. If you want to have sex, have at it. And if you don't feel it, then don't. Do whatever it is that you want to do. No one else calls the shots."

That's the scariest thing of all.

"Maybe I'll see if he still wants to meet about Molly."

Sierra wanted to do a good job on this movie. She liked acting and she wouldn't mind making a career out of it. She had to get better though, and grow as a performer. Ryan Ward could help her with that goal.

He wasn't even interested in her. Not in that way. He simply wanted the movie to be the best it could be. She'd be a fool to think anything else.

CHAPTER
Five

THE MOVIE WASN'T Ryan's taste in the least. Sweet and simple with a romantic all-is-lost moment that could have been resolved with a five-minute conversation, it was a poster child for all that was wrong with films these days. The screenwriter had clearly underestimated the intelligence of the average moviegoer. There was nothing challenging or even different about the lead characters. This boy meets girl story had been done a hundred times and often much better.

It was going to make buckets of money.

Because it hit every trope perfectly. The screenwriter might not think the average moviegoer was very smart but he did know what they wanted to watch. They wanted more of what they already liked but with a slightly different twist, and that he'd delivered on spectacularly. Since he wasn't able to play with the leads much, he'd written two amazingly funny and interesting supporting roles. Roles that Stan, for some unknown reason, had diminished. It didn't make much sense but Ryan was going to right the ship. The scenes and lines that had been cut were going to be restored and this movie might actually be entertaining. He was happy to do Stan a favor but he wasn't going to put his name on a piece of Hollywood mediocrity. He'd promised to do his best and that was exactly what he was going to do.

Deep in studying the script changes, he didn't hear Sierra until she was standing right next to him. He snapped the binder closed to give her his undivided attention. He still couldn't put his finger on why he was so attracted to her. He'd seen more beautiful women, although Sierra was lovely. Maybe it was how she smiled at everyone from the lowliest go-fer on up. She treated everyone the same and that wasn't behavior that he witnessed nearly as much as he should in this business. Everyone - cast and crew - clearly liked her. All except Angela, of course.

And if Angela doesn't like you, you're probably doing something right.

"Sierra, how can I help you?"

The younger woman was dressed in costume for the next take and the wardrobe department had done an excellent job. The scene was for a girl's night out and Sierra was wearing a snazzy red cocktail dress that showed off her long, tanned legs. She must have already been in hair and makeup as well because her brown tresses had been coiled on top of her head with a few curled strands around her face. The hairstyle showed off her perfect bone structure and full lips.

Lips I wouldn't mind...get your mind out of the gutter, man.

Sierra plucked nervously at the belt of her dress. "I was thinking about your offer to help me."

Really? That was interesting news.

"Did you change your mind?"

"Yes, if that's okay. I know that you're really busy." Her head tilted and her brows pinched together. "You look like you didn't get much sleep last night."

Ryan chuckled at her astute observation. "Then I look better than I thought I did because I didn't get *any* sleep last night."

She appeared horrified but he shook his head at her concern. "Seriously, it's okay. I'm one of those weird people that doesn't need much sleep. If I get five or six hours tonight I'll be all caught up."

"That's...good."

But she didn't look convinced. People that slept normally never understood. Sometimes he wished he slept like regular humans but he simply didn't. Luckily, it gave him more time to work on activities he truly enjoyed.

"How about we meet and work over dinner?" he suggested. "There's a really cute cafe called Picasso's in the downtown area. I ate there last night and it was excellent. Quiet, too."

"I know that place. I eat there all the time."

"I'll get with you at the end of the day as to when. I'm not sure how long we'll be working today. Is that okay?"

Sierra smiled, clearly relieved that he was still wanting to help. It was cute that she had been nervous to talk to him about it. "Perfect. And thank you."

"You're welcome."

Ryan watched Sierra walk away instead of putting his

nose back where it belonged - in the script. He was intrigued. Interested. He wasn't the type to fall for a woman easily, so it said something about this female that she'd managed to snag his attention and hadn't let go. He wouldn't mind spending more time with her, getting to know her better.

Who am I kidding? I wouldn't mind going to bed with Sierra Oliver. In fact, I'd like to a lot.

Nothing serious, though. Just a little fun in the sheets between two co-workers. An on-set fling that would bring them both pleasure and leave them with a few happy memories. Was Sierra up for a no-strings affair? She was so new to Hollywood. Did she realize that most of the romances were as fake as the movie sets and the special effects?

Because Ryan might be making a romantic movie, but he didn't believe in happily ever after. This industry had made him too cynical.

————

This isn't a date, so stop acting like it is.

It was actually kind of funny that Sierra was acting this way. She'd barely dated in high school. Brian had basically been her first serious boyfriend, so she had little to no experience with the opposite sex other than her twisted ex.

But the anticipation of seeing Ryan felt the same as she remembered when Tim Hazlett worked up the courage to ask her to the movies when she was fifteen. She'd changed outfits several times, although she didn't have that many clothes to begin with. Billie had curled Sierra's hair and talked to her the whole time, keeping her calm until Tim showed up. Her sister hadn't gone on her first date yet but somehow she'd known just what to say. Later Sierra had told Billie about how Tim had stuck his tongue in her mouth when he'd kissed her goodnight.

Filming had finished around seven which was fairly early, so Sierra had time to take a quick shower and change into jeans and a cream-colored sweater. Her face had been scrubbed of the heavy production makeup and she wanted to let her skin breathe a little so she only added some mascara and lipgloss. No blush was needed as her cheeks were flushed with excitement and more than a bit of nervousness. She pulled her hair back into a ponytail and checked her reflection one last time, making a face in the mirror.

It was going to have to do.

And it's not a date anyway. So it doesn't matter.

But it still kind of felt that way. Sierra couldn't remember the last time she'd been so attracted to a man. If ever. Whenever they were in the same room, she acted like a schoolgirl. Her palms were clammy, her stomach did somersaults, and her lips had trouble forming actual, real words that others could understand.

Billie had suggested that Sierra go for it with Ryan. Flirt, date, have sex. Let herself go and have the fun that she'd missed out on. But that was easier said than done. Not that she needed to worry about this at all.

Ryan wasn't interested in her...that way. Right? But if he was, what was she prepared to do about it?

———

I am sweating through my t-shirt. What the hell is wrong with me?

Grimly, Ryan stomped back into the bedroom of the little condo he was staying in while working on the movie. He needed another damn shirt. Ripping off the white button down, he tossed it on the bed and then tugged the white t-shirt he'd been wearing underneath off and away.

This was ridiculous. He was a grown man but an innocent dinner date with this woman had sent him into a tailspin.

This is not a date. This is business.

Okay, it was business but he'd admitted that he was interested in Sierra Oliver. If the evening ended up in his or her bed he wouldn't be upset.

Checking his armpits one last time, Ryan reached for his deodorant next to the bathroom sink and gave them a quick spritz. They smelled fine but a guy couldn't be too careful. He didn't want Sierra - or anyone - saying that he was stinky. He'd taken a shower when he got home but there wasn't time for another one. His current state was going to have to do.

It doesn't matter. It's not a date, you idiot.

Looking into the mirror, his hand went to his jaw where he was sporting a five o'clock shadow. Shit, should he shave too? Would she notice and think he was trying too hard?

No, he wasn't going to shave. In fact, he was going to run his fingers through his hair and forget about his comb. Because this wasn't a date. He was helping an actress with her role which he'd literally done dozens of times. The fact that he'd ended up in bed with those actresses approximately ninety-seven-point-five percent of the time wasn't something he was even thinking about.

Maybe I should change my shirt.

Fuck it. He whirled away from the mirror and strode out of his condo, flipping off lights and grabbing his coat on the way. He was supposed to meet Sierra in ten minutes at the cafe and it would take eight to walk there. Luckily it wasn't raining tonight, although the temperature was rapidly dropping. Jogging down his front steps, he almost ran into another person on the sidewalk who was bundled up against the cold. He quickly apologized but then stepped back when he recognized who it was.

Sierra, wrapped in a dark wool coat, a bright red scarf, and a script tucked under her arm.

Nobody had told him she was his neighbor. It was like a sign from the universe.

CHAPTER

Six

OVER DINNER SIERRA somehow managed to relax despite Ryan's physical presence only about a foot away. He looked handsome, smelled yummy, and was easy to talk to as well. He was so polite he'd laughed at her lame jokes.

The single glass of wine she'd ordered didn't hurt either. She was impressed by his intelligence and how deeply he understood the characters. Even in this relatively straightforward romantic comedy he'd delved deeply into Molly, writing up what he thought her backstory might be. Then while they were eating, he questioned Sierra about all things Molly-related.

Her favorite flavor of ice cream? Her favorite color? Who was her best friend in school? Was she a good student? What was her favorite subject? Is she rock and roll or country? Would she slap a man if he was handsy or would she just ignore him? The questions went on and on.

By the time dinner was over, Sierra felt like she knew

Molly inside and out. Sometimes she hadn't known the answer right away but she and Ryan would talk it over and decide. Now there wasn't a doubt in her mind as to how Molly would react in any situation. She was absolutely more confident about playing this role and she'd only spent a few hours with him.

You were right, Billie and Tyler. This was a good idea.

"I want to thank you," she said as their plates were being cleared. "Seriously, this has been so helpful. I thought I knew Molly but I had only scratched the surface."

"You're very welcome. It's wonderful to work with someone who wants to go the extra mile with a character. You were doing the work but not all in one session. Instead, you were asking questions piecemeal."

That was true. With each scene she'd analyze what Molly would do and how she would react, but this was far easier. Understanding her whole character made more sense.

"I have a lot to learn," Sierra confessed. "And I appreciate you working with me. This was invaluable and something I'll use going forward."

Ryan shrugged but smiled. "Everyone works differently. Some actors go Method and have to live as the character twenty-four-seven. Some actors are very instinctual and sitting down like this to figure out every detail would appall them. I think you and I are alike in that we like to see the complete picture in front of us. At least I do...I don't want to put words in your mouth."

Sierra didn't get a chance to reply in the affirmative as the waitress returned to their table.

"Any dessert?"

Ryan and Sierra both shook their heads but the smiling server wasn't going to give in easily.

"Are you sure? We have a hot chocolate chip cookie that's baked in a small cast iron skillet and then topped with vanilla ice cream and hot fudge. It's so good."

It sounded delicious and if it had been just her and Billie, Sierra would have ordered it in a split second. But she was here with her director and she didn't want him to think she wasn't going to be able to fit into her costumes the next day.

It looked like Ryan was waffling back and forth, however. Biting his lip and rubbing his chin, he wanted to say yes. Badly.

"You should order it."

He didn't have to be in front of the cameras, after all. He could have ten of them if he wanted to.

"Only if you'll share it with me."

If he only knew just how much she wanted to do that. Or better yet, have one of her very own.

"I shouldn't."

"A few bites." His gaze raked her from head to toe, sending tingling warmth to her extremities. "I bet you work out."

Sierra couldn't stop the laughter that came spilling out of her mouth. "You'd lose your money. I guess you could say I work out. I started a yoga thing with my sister in the last year. Before that I just worked hard. That will keep you in shape whether it was your goal or not."

If anything, Billie and Tyler had been trying to put weight on her, not take it off. She was naturally slim and that was just the genetic lottery. Her life had also been filled with stress, a punishing work schedule, and very little money. It wasn't a recipe for gaining pounds, especially when she barely had time to eat. With their shoestring budget she'd become an expert at buying and preparing nutritious food that didn't cost an arm and a leg. In other words, she'd cooked a lot of beans.

"Then we're definitely getting this dessert. We'll take one, thank you."

The waitress bustled back into the kitchen and Ryan turned his attention back to Sierra. It was a little disconcerting the way he gave her his total concentration. He could probably make anyone think they were the only person in the room. Maybe it was a trait that directors needed.

"Since we've done our work for the evening, why don't you tell me a little more about yourself? You said you worked hard. What kind of work did you do?"

He wasn't going to give up asking questions about her life. Not that she was ashamed of her life - she wasn't. She'd gone through some terrible crap and come out the other side a stronger person. It had been hard accepting help from her sister and Tyler but deep down she'd known it was the only way to get away from her heinous ex-husband.

The story, however, sounded so sad and melodramatic. She didn't want people to think of her as a victim or that she was trying to get their sympathy. She didn't want or need that. Therapy had gone a long way to helping her be in a healthy headspace and wallowing in the past hoping for pats on the head from others wasn't her style.

She didn't want to lie though, so she decided to tell the truth. Selectively. "I was a waitress. It's pretty physical work, carrying heavy trays. You're on your feet the entire time. I always tip well."

"The image of the struggling actress doing waitress duty is almost an institution," Ryan mused. "Did you always want to be an actress?"

"No," she answered honestly. "It never occurred to me until Sam Collins brought it up when I worked as Billie's assistant on their movie. He heard me running lines with her."

"Sam has an excellent eye for talent. So if you didn't want to be an actress when you grew up, what did you want to be?"

It was a funny question as Sierra could barely remember being a child. With an alcoholic mother, she'd felt old by the time she went to school. She'd had a rich fantasy life and it had always consisted of having a happy family and a mother and father who loved her and kissed her goodnight.

I wanted to be loved.

"Maybe that was my problem," Sierra replied instead. "I didn't know what I wanted to be."

Dreams were expensive. They wasted time when a human is trying to simply survive.

His head tilted to the side, as if trying to see inside of her thoughts. "Why do I get the feeling you're avoiding my questions? You can tell me it's none of my business, you know."

Because I am avoiding your questions.

"I don't like talking about my life," she confessed. "It

wasn't exactly 'The Brady Bunch'. It wasn't even 'Roseanne'."

"More like an afterschool special?" he asked softly. "I get it. Not a great childhood."

"It was bad and then I made a couple of stupid decisions and managed to make things worse."

So vague.

"I doubt that. You seem like a smart woman."

He didn't know the half of it.

"This is hard-won street smarts you're seeing. But I made some stupid moves earlier in my life. I trusted the wrong people."

Ryan didn't reply at once but he did nod as if he understood. He didn't, though. He just thought he did.

"A man?" he finally asked.

Sierra raised her glass as if in toast. "The oldest story in the book. My man done did me wrong."

The waitress interrupted by sliding their dessert onto the middle of the table along with two spoons. Sierra could smell the heavenly sweet aroma of melted chocolate and vanilla. Steam rose from the just baked cookie and her mouth watered despite her full tummy. She had a big sweet tooth and this was ticking every box on her yummy list.

They each took a big bite and Sierra closed her eyes at the pleasure that spread across her taste buds. She had a little bit of the gooey warm cookie and a little bit of the cool vanilla ice cream and it was perfection.

"Damn, that's good," Ryan said, wiping at his sticky lips with a paper napkin. "I love chocolate. I could eat it all day."

"Me too," Sierra agreed, helping herself to another big bite. Any ideas of propriety or shame had gone out of the window. She was going to eat part of this dessert and opinions be damned. "There is nothing like a warm chocolate chip cookie. It should be a food group all its own."

"My mom made the best chocolate chip cookies. I asked her what the secret ingredient was and you know what she said?"

"Love," Sierra replied promptly.

Ryan just laughed. "You'd think that would be it but she said it was a teaspoon of orange peel. To this day, that's how I make them."

"You can make cookies?"

"Hell, yes. A man has to have a few tricks up his sleeve when it comes to romancing the ladies. Home baked cookies are usually a hit." He leaned forward, his blue eyes sparkling. "Women have perfume and lingerie. Some men have displays of manly prowess in sports. But I'm just a big geek so I use cooking. I can make a three-course meal and never break a sweat."

He didn't look domesticated. "You're a gourmet cook? For real?"

He held up his hands in surrender. "Whoa, whoa, whoa. Who said anything about gourmet? I said I could cook. I specialize in comfort foods. I wouldn't say anything I made was high brow. My favorite thing to eat is cheeseburgers. What's yours?"

"I love cheeseburgers but I'd have to say my favorite food is spaghetti and meatballs. Can you make that?"

"I absolutely can. Maybe I can make you dinner one night?"

He'd asked casually enough but Sierra was fine-tuned to his every word and expression. It hadn't been an empty offer. He was serious. Immediately that awkward feeling was back, and he could tell. Her cheeks were warm with embarrassment and she suddenly didn't know where to look or what to say. He'd taken her off guard.

"Am I making you uncomfortable?" he finally asked, placing his spoon on a small plate. "This isn't a quid pro quo thing, Sierra. I like you and I'm interested in you, but if you don't feel the same it's fine. We'll still work together and it's all good. I'd just be lying if I said that I only want to be your director."

She didn't want him to think that there was anything wrong with him. This was her issue.

"I–I haven't dated in awhile."

That was an understatement the size of the Grand Canyon.

"That man who did you wrong? He's the reason?"

She nodded, not sure what to say or how much to reveal. "Let's just say it didn't end well. It wasn't a...healthy relationship."

"Were you with him long?"

Way too long.

"Since high school," she admitted uncomfortably under his scrutiny. If he knew the truth, would he think less of her? That somehow she'd allowed herself to be beaten down and demoralized to the point where she couldn't leave an abusive man? The truth was her ex had convinced her that it was all her fault and that she deserved it. "I finally left him almost two years ago."

"That's a long time."

It appeared that Ryan didn't know what to say either. It was clear she wasn't telling the whole truth but it didn't look like he wanted to try and force her to say things she wasn't ready to reveal. They were both walking on eggshells except she was the only one that knew why.

"I missed a lot," she said, uncomfortable speaking about this. "I haven't dated much in my life. I've barely been anywhere. I have a list of things that I'd like to do, though."

That seemed to peak his interest because he was completely ignoring their melting dessert, instead training his gaze on her. "You mean like a bucket list?"

"Sort of, but it's more a list of things I didn't get to do. Although I have to say that it's grown into a list of stuff I just want to do but didn't necessarily miss. For example, Billie and I went to the top of the Eiffel Tower. That isn't anything that I missed per se, but it was an item I'd placed on my list when we were working in Paris."

"That sounds wonderful." Ryan pursed his lips, pinching at them with his thumb and forefinger. "What else is on that list?"

Sierra laughed at the question. "I'm not stupid, Ryan. There's no way I'm going to answer that."

He gave her a charming smile. "C'mon, you can tell me. I won't laugh or anything."

"I never thought you would. It's just that the list is private."

"You can't tell me one thing on that list? What the hell is on it? It must be wild."

He was getting the wrong idea. She wasn't an adrenaline junkie.

"I don't want to bungee jump or anything. I just want to

have some fun. Have the kind of experiences that most young women take for granted."

"Like party and drink? Go dancing and flirt with men?"

Lifting a shoulder in a shrug, she took another bite of their dessert. "Not those things specifically but you kind of get the idea."

"What else?" Ryan pressed, his own spoon forgotten.

He was like a dog with a bone. She needed to close down this conversation.

"I want to go dancing and see plays. I want to go to the beach and just generally enjoy myself. I am not in any way, shape or form looking for a relationship. I don't want to get serious with anyone. I just want to date casually. I don't want to fall in love. I just want to meet a lot of people and go out and live my life. So that is what's on my list."

"I can do that."

She didn't know what he meant.

"Pardon?"

"I can do that, Sierra."

"You can do what?"

"Be casual. Not be serious. In fact, that's what I want, too. Isn't that perfect? We both want the same thing."

It was not perfect. Not even close. Was he proposing that they date casually?

"I guess we do," she replied cautiously. "I'm not sure why that's perfect, though."

Ryan was smiling now, and he was very handsome when he was happy like this.

"I asked you out on a date, Sierra. You didn't say no."

She shoved the cookie away. "I didn't say yes, either."

"You said that you hadn't dated in awhile. You also said

that you wanted to meet people and have fun." His brows rose and he grinned evilly. "I'm fun. Everyone says so."

"No, they don't," Sierra gasped. "They say that you're mean and you make people cry on set."

"Only the people that deserve it. So what do you say? How about I cook you dinner one night?"

It was a bad idea on so many levels. He didn't understand that he was a Harley and she needed training wheels. It would be like a student driver taking a Lamborghini for a spin.

Not a good idea.

"I don't think it's a good idea."

To his credit, he didn't badger her or try to start a negotiation. He immediately backed off, to her total relief. She probably would have given in if he'd pressed the subject.

"Okay, but just know that the offer is open if you ever change your mind."

"I won't. I think we should keep this strictly professional."

"If you say so."

"I do. It's for the best."

Except that she didn't sound sure even to herself. There was a part of her - a huge part - that wanted to say yes. She had a feeling that Ryan Ward knew how to have more fun than she'd ever imagined.

CHAPTER
Seven

IT WAS like winning the lottery but losing the ticket.

Sierra wanted the same thing Ryan did. Have a casual relationship. Have some fun but not get too serious or tied down with messy emotions and commitment. If commitment was so wonderful, they'd have a better word for it.

But she'd turned him down flat. There had been no equivocation in her tone when she'd said no and he knew good and well that persuasion wasn't a great idea. In fact, he couldn't remember the last time he'd had to convince a woman to date him. They usually came on to him. It had been a long time since his ego had taken a battering. Perhaps the last time was when a critic said Ryan had the cinematic vision of a slug.

They tussled over the check when the waitress dropped it off but somehow he'd managed to wrestle it out of her hands and pay it. It might not be a date but he'd invited her, so he wanted to pick up the bill. It wasn't a big deal, which was what he told Sierra. She'd given in but the mutinous set of her lips had him thinking that this wasn't the last he was going to hear about this.

"Let me help you on with your coat."

She murmured a thank you as he held her wool coat up and she slid her arms in. They'd only been standing next to one another for a few seconds but he'd caught a whiff of her shampoo and it smelled like summer, a mix of coconut and sunshine. Geez, these cosmetic companies were really getting crafty with their aromas. Some poor bastard who wasn't as savvy as he was would easily fall into the trap thinking the female was as wonderful as a sunny day at the beach.

Although Sierra is fantastic.

Both of them bundled up against the cold, they headed down the sidewalk and toward the condo development where they were both living. Neither of them spoke; maybe because they'd already said everything or maybe because it was freezing outside and their teeth were chattering. The temperature had dropped at least twenty degrees in the last few hours.

The walk home took exactly the same amount of time as the walk there but it felt much longer. Sierra's cheeks were bright red and she had her gloved hands shoved in the pockets of her coat as they hurried back, the path lit only by streetlights. As much as he wanted to spend more time with her they were both relieved when their homes were in sight. He was a California boy and he didn't do cold.

He followed her up to her door and waited while she fumbled in her purse for the keys. Quickly unlocking the door, she turned back to him and suddenly it felt like a date again with a pounding heart and sweaty palms despite the temperature.

The drop off at the door. This was when he was supposed to get a kiss, right?

No kiss for you, asshole. This isn't a date. She said no.

"Thank you for all of your help tonight," she said, her fingers playing with the keyring. "I feel much more confident about playing Molly now and I couldn't have done that without you."

"You're welcome." His voice felt rusty but he put it down to the biting wind. "There's still a few more scenes to go through."

So let's do this again.

"I can't ask you to spend more time helping me. I know you're a busy man."

"This is important. We'll find the time."

The conversation dwindled as they both stood there, seemingly unsure as to what to do next. The tension between them had built to an almost unbearable level. He was supposed to turn and leave, maybe wave as he headed into his own condo but his feet were firmly planted on her front stoop. For some reason, he couldn't make himself walk away and eventually it was going to get mighty awkward.

Did she feel it too or was he all alone in his quandary? He was a like a teenage boy out of his depth and nervous as he bid goodnight to his first date. But this wasn't Ryan's first date. He was a grown man who had lost count of the women who had drifted in and out of his life. Surely Sierra would be no different in the long run. Six months from now he'd remember her as sweet and beautiful but the details would have blurred.

That didn't explain, however, why he was standing here freezing his nuts off with this female.

This girl isn't interested. Move along.

Her eyes finally met his and he watched fascinated as she licked her lips. "And thank you for dinner. You really didn't have to pick up the check."

"I was happy to."

Their bodies seemed to sway toward one another, their gazes locked. Ryan didn't inhale or exhale, terrified to break the spell that the old-fashioned yellow porch light had cast over them. He searched her green-gold eyes for some sign that she was in the same predicament. His gaze dropped to her lips, shiny and full and incredibly tempting. If he allowed himself to move just an inch or two closer they'd be kissing.

He didn't move and neither did she, trapped in their own indecision. At least he was.

The moment lasted for one heartbeat...two...three...

Then it was over as quickly as it had begun. This time it was Sierra who made the big move, pushing open her front door and flicking on the switch so that light flooded her living room. She stepped inside and away so there was nothing more for him to say or do. The evening had come to an end.

Time to leave, buddy.

"Goodnight, Ryan. Thank you again."

"Night, Sierra. See you tomorrow."

He didn't bother to go down the stairs to the sidewalk and then up to his own porch, instead walking across the tiny front yard to his own condo. He could hear her front door click close and he stood and waited until he heard the deadbolt safely engage before entering his own home.

All by himself. He'd better get used to it, at least during this movie shoot because Sierra Oliver wasn't interested in him in the least.

―――――

Letting out the breath she'd been holding, Sierra leaned back against the closed door. She'd been so close to making a fool of herself and kissing Ryan. There was something about him, a pull she couldn't deny. She'd learned tonight that not only was he incredibly handsome, he was intelligent and funny, too. It was a trifecta that was hard to ignore. Add in the kindness that he displayed and it was no wonder she was attracted to him.

He is out of your league, girl.

But wouldn't it be fun?

She'd done the right thing turning him down for a date. He played by a whole different set of rules. From what she'd heard he was a master at *love 'em and leave 'em*. It would be crazy to get involved with a professional heartbreaker like Ryan Ward.

If this was the right thing to do, why did it feel so crappy?

CHAPTER
Eight

THE NEXT DAY Sierra tried to hide out in her trailer but that was proving to be difficult as Ryan was shooting scenes she was in. The same scenes they'd worked on last night.

When she'd almost made a fool of herself.

She'd tossed and turned for quite awhile wondering what might have happened if she'd given in to her urge. He was clearly attracted to her, evidenced by his invitation to dinner. He probably would have kissed her back. Then maybe he would have wanted to come inside her condo. They would have kissed some more and that might have led to them heading to her bedroom. And that's where the whole thing became complicated.

Ryan Ward dated glamorous sexy women whom Sierra would bet knew a thing or two about how to please a man. She, on the other hand, didn't know shit. Her ex hadn't exactly given a crap about her pleasure and he'd basically climbed on top of her and pumped a few times before grunting, rolling off, and falling instantly asleep. In the beginning there had been lots of necking and that had been nice but once he'd gotten her in bed that all stopped. Foreplay had been almost nonexistent. The only reason she knew anything at all about sex was from the novels she'd read through the years and the conversations she'd had with other women.

If she slept with Ryan, he'd figure out that she didn't have a clue between the sheets. Once again, she needed to start slow. Find a nice guy who didn't have the sexual history of James Bond. Frankly, it was intimidating to think she might be evaluated and found wanting.

Since hiding was out, Sierra tried to keep her nose in a book as much as possible. They were on location today, shooting a few scenes outside. Sierra, Angela, and one of the other costars were supposed to walk down the sidewalk arguing about whether the heroine should give the hero a second chance. Luckily, the weather was mild today with the temperature hovering around forty degrees. A girl from Wisconsin, Sierra considered it balmy weather but Ryan clearly didn't share her feelings. Between every take, while they'd reset the equipment he'd disappear into his trailer to warm up, which might have made her laugh under different circumstances.

It didn't help either that Angela kept finding reasons to follow him. She needed to talk about her character's motivation, or she needed to discuss a particular line of dialogue that she might want to improvise. Normally Ryan didn't have much patience with Angela's antics but today he appeared to be allowing it, not barking or growling at her as he'd done in the past. This last time they were staying in the trailer quite a long time. The crew was ready but Ryan and Angela hadn't reemerged yet. Everyone was beginning to get antsy and of course, the speculation began in earnest.

Just what was going on in there?

Her costar Tony sidled up to her, a smirk on his face. "Knowing Ryan's reputation we could all be waiting awhile."

Sierra didn't look up from her book. This situation didn't bother her because she wasn't jealous.

"I'm sure they're discussing the scene."

Laughing out loud, Tony shook his head. "Sure, that's what they're doing. Because this scene with her walking down the street is so complex. She wants her character's motivation. Didn't he tell her yesterday that her motivation was to get the goddamn take before the end of the day?"

Ryan had indeed done just that and Sierra had enjoyed that smackdown of the leading lady immensely. Angela grated on Sierra's nerves even when she wasn't flirting with Ryan.

Okay, maybe I'm a little jealous.

"I'm sure they'll be out in a moment."

I hope. What are they doing in there?

"What Angela wants Angela gets, and she wants Ward. If she plays her cards right, maybe she'll get a real role in his next movie. The kind that get awards."

With a huff, Sierra closed her book. "That's a horrible thing to do to someone. He doesn't deserve to be used like that."

Tony frowned and then chuckled. "You're such a newbie. You'd think with your connections in the business you'd be a little more savvy. That's how things work, little girl. You scratch my back and I'll scratch yours. Besides, I doubt that poor Ryan is being used and abused by Angela. I'm guessing he'll leave that trailer with a smile on his face."

The ugly truth about Hollywood was that it was often about who you knew rather than what you knew. Sometimes it was as simple as having a friend in the right place, sometimes it was as seedy as being...*friendly* to the right person. Sierra wanted nothing to do with it. If she had to debase herself to get a part, then she wouldn't get it. She wasn't willing to do anything unprofessional to make it in this business. If that meant she never acted again, so be it. Frankly, this was all a lark anyway.

I still can't believe anyone thinks I can act.

The door to Ryan's trailer was still firmly closed a few minutes later when Sierra's phone rang. Tony had wandered off when she wouldn't gossip with him, so she tucked her book away for the second time and checked her cell.

Billie.

Probably making sure Sierra was okay. As twins they had a sort of spooky connection and when one wasn't feeling quite right the other felt it as well.

"Hey, aren't you supposed to be working?"

Tyler and Billie were working on a movie together. Their first joint project and they were having a ball doing it. They wanted to be the next Hepburn and Tracey.

Billie's groan could be heard loud and clear through the phone. "Is your set as boring as ours? They're messing with the lighting and I swear I was younger when they started."

Sierra's gaze flickered to Ryan's trailer. Door still closed.

"Sort of. We're also in between takes. What's going on? How's Tyler?"

Sierra adored her brother-in-law. He was funny and protective and he'd always been honest with her. The fact that he worshipped the ground Billie walked on didn't hurt either.

"He's fine. He loves making a movie where he gets to keep his shirt on. He ate carbs last night and I swear he had an orgasm by the time he finished his spaghetti. It was almost obscene."

"Is he planning on losing that six-pack?"

Tyler Gaylord was known for being hot and sexy in the *Thunder* movies. He'd graced many a magazine cover and usually his bare torso was on full display, much to many women's delight.

"I hope not because he, Sam, Max, and Nate are making a movie after this one and he needs to be in shape. He may not have to take off his clothes but the shoot will be physical. I'd hate to see him get injured because he didn't prepare."

"But you don't care about the abs."

Billie giggled. "Well, they don't hurt, that's for sure, but I'd love him no matter what. Now tell me what's going on with that hottie director of yours. Did you accept his offer of help?"

Another glance at Ryan's trailer. No change.

This was actually sort of humiliating and she felt the anger churn in her stomach. He'd asked Sierra out less than twenty-four hours ago and now he was playing hide-the-Oscar with that skank Angela. He wasn't any different than the usual Hollywood snake. She'd been fooled by his charming smile.

"I did."

"And did he help you? Did you meet with him?"

Boy, did I.

"Last night we worked over dinner."

Sierra's brevity must have set off warning bells in her sister's head. "I see. Did it not go well? Did he...try something? Because you just kick them in the balls, sis. Don't put up with that crap for a second. In fact, I'll tell Tyler and he'll kick Ryan Ward's ass."

Sierra inwardly groaned. That's all she needed was Tyler and a few of his friends to rough up Ryan. What a mess.

"He didn't try anything so put your hubby in your holster and calm down. We ate dinner, we worked. That's it. Nothing to report here."

Except that I wanted to kiss him. Badly.

There was silence on the other end and for a moment Sierra thought the call had dropped.

"You're lying. You can never lie to me. Other people? Yes, but not me."

That was the problem with having a twin. They knew you as well or better than you knew yourself.

"I'm attracted to him." It hurt to admit it. "But it's not a big deal."

"He's not attracted to you? Then he has lousy taste in women."

There was no point in trying to keep anything from Billie. She'd get it out of Sierra eventually.

"He asked me out. He offered to make dinner for me."

"And...you said...yes? Or no? Help me here because I'm confused."

So am I. Join the club.

"I said no. I didn't think it was a good idea to get involved with him."

"Oh." Billie for once didn't have much to day. "I see. May I ask why?"

Since when did her sister ask for permission?

"It's what I said before. He's so far out of my league," Sierra sighed. "Like way out. I'm playing Little League and he's at Wrigley Field."

"You give yourself too little credit. You're awesome."

"I'm a rookie. He's expect me to know the game but I've never played."

"Then make up your own rules," Billie snorted. "Don't play by his. You be in control. You're not looking for a big relationship, right?"

Heavens, no.

"Absolutely not."

"Then lay down the law before he has a chance to. Seize the day and all of that jazz. He's perfect for a quick fling. You'll have some fun and then move on to your next job. The ending is built in so there won't be any declarations of love and weepy angst. There are no decisions to make, no wondering what might happen when the film wraps. It's the ideal fling situation."

Billie was speaking as if from experience. "And just how many of these flings have you had, sister dear?"

"I might have had one or two before I fell for Tyler," Billie admitted. "I wasn't a virgin but you practically are.

That ex of yours wasn't doing his job, but I bet Ryan Ward knows what to do."

Sierra glanced at the trailer door. Still closed.

Without a doubt, Ryan knew what to do in the bedroom. The problem was he was currently doing it with his leading lady. If he could go from her to Angela that quickly, she'd made the right decision last night.

But it still kind of hurt.

CHAPTER
Nine

RYAN GROWLED INTO THE PHONE, barely managing not to slam the electronic device repeatedly against the kitchen table until it was a useless hunk of metal. He was frustrated and the man on the other end of the line was trying to explain the situation as patiently as possible.

"It's an Act of God, Ryan," Daryl Woods, the production manager, said. "You can't film when the city doesn't want cars or people on the roads. It's a goddamn ice storm and it's dangerous."

A world covered in ice wasn't something Ryan was used to. He was Southern California born and bred, comfortable at the beach. Sure, he'd gone skiing any number of times but he couldn't remember a time that he'd been trapped inside of his lodgings because a thin, frozen layer of water had covered his surroundings.

"They don't know how bad it's really going to be," Ryan

argued. "It's not even here yet. It might be just fine tomorrow."

The storm was predicted to show up this afternoon and the little college town had urged everyone to close up early and get home before the streets became skating rinks.

"Or it might not." Daryl's tone was becoming less pleasant by the second. "You can't take chances with people's lives. The studio will under–"

"The studio will roast my balls over an open fire," Ryan shot back. "They don't give a shit about Acts of God. They only care about the budget and schedule."

"That got blown to hell when Stan had a heart attack. They should be on their knees in thanks that you even took this job. Now, for the love of all that's good and holy, wrap up shooting for the day and call off for tomorrow. I don't want our permits yanked by the town council because they had to call out the police or an ambulance when we didn't follow directions."

That was a real possibility. Cities loathed and loved having a film crew in town. They wanted the money that it pushed into the local economy but the disruptions weren't as popular. Ryan had always prided himself on being as unobtrusive as possible.

"Fine," Ryan finally conceded. This wasn't a fight he was going to win. "But somehow we're going to make this up in the schedule. I'm not sure how but we will."

Their fourteen-hour days just became eighteen hours. It was only for a few more weeks. Everyone would survive. They'd bitch and moan and call him a bastard...but they'd live.

"I'm beginning to understand why you're so popular

among the cast and crew you've worked with," Daryl said sarcastically. "You're a real sweetheart."

"They hate me until they see the final product. Then I'm a genius. Besides, I'd never ask them to do anything I'm not willing to do myself."

"I'll call you tomorrow," Daryl promised. "I'll let you know the latest from the town council."

An ice storm in March. According to the locals around him, this wasn't unheard of, although it was unusual. It happened once a decade and here it was. His timing sucked.

"Burt," he called to his assistant director who was hovering nearby pretending not to listen in. "Let's finish getting this scene and then close it down for the day. We won't be filming tomorrow, either."

The actors were seemingly motivated to have some time off even if it meant being stuck in their homes. The next few takes went off without a hitch and by three o'clock they had finished for the day. Ryan was one of the last to leave and he locked his trailer behind him before climbing into his rented vehicle.

He gave one last look around, hoping to spot Sierra but she must have left before lunch since her scenes were done. She'd been difficult to speak to the last few days, always surrounded by others. He really wanted to talk to her, just the two of them. He wouldn't press her to go out on a date with him - she'd made her feelings clear about that - but he simply wanted to spend some time with her. They'd had fun the other night. She was so smart and funny, not at all like his nightmare of a leading lady Angela.

Holy hell, that woman should come with a warning label and a bottle of Valium. No wonder Stan had collapsed on the set. She'd been driving Ryan crazy for two days, asking question after question about her character, her motivation, her dialogue. Anything and everything she could think of so that her ass was planted in his trailer between takes. He wasn't an idiot. He knew good and well what Angela wanted. She wasn't going to get it, though. He'd rather kiss a snake. With tongue.

The temperature was dropping rapidly so he was glad to be back in his little condo less than fifteen minutes later. The rain was falling steadily now and according to the weather report on the radio, it was all going to turn to ice overnight making driving conditions treacherous. All citizens were advised to stay the hell home.

Tired to the bone from trying to get the picture back on schedule, Ryan fell back onto the couch and flipped on the television. Daytime television sucked. There was nothing on but talk shows and old reruns. He settled on an episode of "Leave it to Beaver" and settled back to watch the Beav getting in trouble for some little thing that most parents wouldn't give a shit about. And that Eddie Haskell needed to get his ass kicked.

At some point Ryan must have drifted off because when he woke the room was dark and the television was quiet. The condo was chilly and he pulled the throw from the back of the sofa around his shoulders as he stood to check the thermostat. The temperature must have really dropped outside for the house to be this cold.

I don't remember turning off the television. Or this lamp.

Reaching for the switch, he turned it several times - the

click loud in the silence - but the lamp didn't turn on. Same with the television, the lamp on the other end table, and every light switch in the house. The power was out.

The house was cold and quiet except for the sound of the rain on the roof. He was safe indoors but for how long? No heat. Barely any food, and with the power off it would all spoil anyway.

Son of a bitch.

———

Bundled up in her coat, hat, and gloves, Sierra stirred the tomato sauce bubbling on the little camp stove she'd purchased at a big box store yesterday. She'd set it up on the screened-in back patio since there was no way she was going to use it indoors. Her cheeks were cold and rosy but she was keeping warm sipping a relaxing glass of wine while stirring the pasta and sauce.

Growing up in Wisconsin, she'd been in more than a few snow and ice storms, so she'd assumed the power would go off. Since her scenes had finished early yesterday, she'd headed out to buy supplies to get through, not wanting to be cold and hungry for twenty-four to thirty-six hours. Most of the bread and milk was gone, but she'd bought that earlier in the week on a regular shopping trip. Instead, she'd picked up a few staples and some storm must-haves too, like marshmallows for roasting over the fire.

The little two-burner propane camp stove had been her best purchase and now she wouldn't have to eat cold food for two days.

"I thought I smelled food. Woman, what are you doing?"

The sound of Ryan's voice had her whirling around to find him standing just outside of her patio door. He was wearing a scowl as if she had offended him deeply. She'd been trying to give him a wide berth the last few days and for the most part it had worked. He'd been so busy and she'd made sure not to be alone as much as possible.

What does it look like I'm doing? Making origami swans?

"I'm cooking dinner," she explained, turning back to her red sauce. He looked absolutely delicious as well, dressed in jeans, a t-shirt, and an oversized brown coat. "What are you doing? You should be careful walking around. It's slick out there."

Ryan opened the screen door and strode in so he was right next to her. He leaned down and took a huge whiff of tomato and garlic.

"That smells amazing. But how are you cooking it? The power is out."

Sierra pointed to the propane canister on the floor. "Propane. It's a camp stove. Haven't you ever been camping?"

He shook his head, still sniffing the sauce. "No, and I wasn't a Boy Scout either. Did this stove come with the condo? Do you think I have one, too?"

Clearly, the man was hungry. And lost as to what to do when the power was out. Seriously, how did these millionaires function by themselves?

"Doubtful. I bought this yesterday when I saw the weather forecast, along with some food."

"No point in buying food," he shrugged. "Power's out. It will just go bad."

He was so handsome and sexy, yet he didn't have a clue.

"Ryan, we can make ice easily and place it in the freezer to keep the food cold, not that I have that much perishable stuff. But it should keep what we have cold until we hopefully get power back tomorrow or the next day."

"You've thought of everything. You'll have food and I guess we can huddle around the stove for warmth."

We? When did I become we?

You know you have to invite him to stay for dinner. It's only polite. He'll starve without you.

"Or you can light a fire in the fireplace," she suggested. "That's what I did."

He frowned again. "You have wood?"

"I had some delivered. There was an ad in the local paper."

Sierra couldn't let Ryan freeze and starve to death. His well-being was far more important than her emotional comfort. She couldn't make this about her. Time to woman up.

"I have enough food for two," she said. "And you're welcome to stay with me. You know...if you want to. It's not super warm but it's better than what you'd have at your place."

Ryan stepped back and shook his head. "I don't want to intrude. I'll be fine on my own."

But he was looking longingly at the sauce.

"You're not intruding. It will be nice to have the company. The pasta should be done so I'll take this inside and strain it. Why don't you go get your things next door and then come over? We can eat and then roast marshmallows for dessert."

It must have been the mention of marshmallows that did it because a grin crossed his face and he bounded away with a cheery, "Thanks, I'll be right back."

I am so stupid, but I couldn't send him away. We'd find his body in the spring thaw.

Sierra was going to spend the twenty-four hours or more alone in an intimate space with a man she lusted after.

What could possibly go wrong?

CHAPTER
Ten

RYAN WAS a man with a healthy appetite. Between the two of them they'd managed to finish off all the pasta plus half of the crusty loaf of bread Sierra had picked up at the bakery downtown. Over dinner he'd regaled her of tales from the movie sets he'd been on while she listened mesmerized to the behind the scenes stories of some of her favorite stars.

"Wait," Sierra said, sitting up from where she was lounging in the front of the fire. They'd built a mound of pillows and eaten dinner there. "You were an actor? I had no idea."

Chuckling, Ryan stretched out more comfortably. "I did always want to be a director but I did some acting jobs early in my career so I could see things from both sides. Believe me when I say that I prefer being behind the camera."

"When the power comes back on, I'm going to search for those movies and rent them. I must see this."

She had to admit to a certain curiosity about how Ryan looked almost twenty years ago.

"Then don't blink. Because in a couple of those master-pieces, my screen time is almost nothing. I'm not complaining, though. I think it's probably best that no one thinks about me when they remember those movies." He leaned forward so they were almost nose to nose. She could smell his aftershave mixed with the oak scent of the burning wood. "In other words, they sucked. Really badly. I wasn't much better. I think the entire industry is better for me being retired from acting."

Sierra sipped at her wine, enjoying its warmth in her belly. "What was your first big break?"

He thought about her question before answering it immediately, his fingertip tapping his chin. "I don't know if it was my big break but it was a milestone for me. I directed a short in film school that caught the attention of a few people in the business. I didn't get a job out of it but they basically encouraged me to keep going. It was just the thing I needed at the time. I was becoming rapidly disillusioned with the movie business. You know how it is."

Technically...no, she didn't. Sierra hadn't said a word but her expression must have told the story.

"You don't know how it is," Ryan replied, laughter in his tone. "Well, let me tell you it's a jungle out there. A real dog eat dog kind of profession."

"I have seen it," she protested, not wanting to seem like she'd used her contacts and friends. "It's just I've been lucky enough to not have experienced it."

"You don't have anything to apologize for, honey. Show business is all about who you know, and you know some powerful people. There's no shame in that. If you weren't any good, you wouldn't have snagged this part. You absolutely would have gotten the audition, but they wouldn't have cast you. You're good."

She felt the heat rush to her cheeks at his compliment. That was something she wasn't sure she would ever get used to hearing. Kind words were an item that she and Billie didn't get much of growing up, nor had Sierra found them with her ex.

Did he realize he called me honey? I kind of like that.

"Thank you. I've been very lucky."

It seemed better to not make a big deal about it.

Ryan refilled his own glass and held up the bottle but she shook her head. As pleasant as this was she needed to keep a clear head on her shoulders. She didn't want to make a fool of herself, which was entirely possible if she had too much to drink.

"You and Billie are twins, right?"

"We are, although not identical."

That was pretty obvious but some people didn't get the distinction regarding one egg compared to two separate ones.

"That must have been great growing up. You had a built-in friend. I bet you're really close. Are you the kind of twins who know what the other is thinking and feeling? Would you know if Billie was hurt or sick?"

Yes, but it isn't as great as it sounds. Feeling someone else's emotions is creepy.

"It was nice," she replied instead. Talking about her childhood wasn't high on her to-do list. "Billie is the best sister ever."

"I've never met Tyler but he seems like a good guy. I have met Sam Collins and Nate Mason, though. All solid actors. Did you know I almost directed the last *Thunder* picture? We couldn't work out the scheduling, though."

Sierra could see Ryan hanging out with Tyler and his friends. They were very much alike.

"They would have liked that but be warned they like to play practical jokes on set."

Ryan threw back his head and laughed. "I've heard about a few of them. I might have a few up my sleeve as well. I grew up in a house of five brothers. You had to be ruthless to survive."

He'd already spoken about his childhood in Southern California. It sounded idyllic to Sierra, who hadn't had the best upbringing. Two parents that loved him. Security. A warm home and food on the table.

"As the middle child I would have thought you wouldn't get involved in shenanigans like that."

His smile was evil and he waggled his eyebrows. "I was the worst of all of them but I was good at blaming it on all of my siblings. No one ever suspects the middle child. We pretend we're quiet but inside..."

"You're a troublemaker," she finished for him. "You wanted the attention you didn't get in your childhood?"

She'd asked the question in jest but his smile told her she was on the money.

"Hell, yeah. But I want the attention on my terms. Being a famous actor isn't my thing, so I guess it's lucky for me I didn't have any talent. Now directing, that's something I love and I get just enough attention for it. What about you? Did you get enough attention as a child, Sierra?"

She'd heard all the theories about actors and actresses. How they craved external approval and were riddled with insecurities. She'd spoken at length to her therapist about it and they'd concluded that she liked having an avenue to channel her emotions whether happy, sad, angry, or hurt. It was a safe avenue for her but mostly she simply enjoyed inhabiting another person, if only for a little while. She liked seeing the world through their eyes, figuring out how they would respond to a situation. It didn't hurt that she had years of hurt, fear, and disappointment to tap to bring the characters to life.

He'd opened up to her, so she didn't want to be rude. In the last few hours, she'd felt closer to him than she had almost anyone since she'd left Wisconsin.

"I wouldn't say that my childhood was any sort of blue-print for a healthy adulthood. As for attention, that's something that Billie and I didn't want from our mother. It was never a good thing."

His smile fell and he frowned, his brow furrowed as he appeared to digest her reply.

"I've never heard Billie talk about her childhood in interviews. I'm guessing that it wasn't a good one."

"It wasn't," Sierra confirmed, finding that it wasn't as difficult as she'd imagined to tell him. In fact, it felt rather freeing. She didn't have anything to be ashamed about. Her mother's failings weren't Sierra's. "My mother had a drinking problem and my father left soon after we were born."

His expression was sympathetic but not pitying, a fact

she appreciated. She didn't want his pity. She didn't want anyone's pity.

I'm not a victim. I'm a survivor.

"Christ, I'm so sorry, honey. That must have been tough, growing up like that. So did you and Billie leave home for Hollywood together?"

And just when she thought she was on solid ground, the earth moved under her and she was weak-kneed like a newborn colt. That question was a loaded one. Ryan didn't have a clue.

I could tell him.

But I haven't told anyone.

Maybe that's why I should.

It's not my fault. I shouldn't have to hide and lie.

But he might not understand. He might think you're weak. He might blame you for not leaving.

If he does, then I'll know who he truly is.

"No," she finally answered, realizing she'd left a long silence in the air. "Billie left but I stayed in Wisconsin. I had...a boyfriend. I later married him. That was a mistake. I should have left with Billie."

Short. To the point. Few details. He might just take it at face value and move on with the conversation.

Ryan sighed and scraped his hand down his face. "And that's why you turned me down when I asked you out? You just got out of a bad marriage? I hope you didn't think I was pressuring you. I'm not like that. I just really like you. Christ, I can't seem to get the words out right. If I had known you'd just split up with your husband, I wouldn't have–I wouldn't have asked you out."

She had to admire his ego. It was certainly healthy as a

horse. He didn't think she'd turned him down because she wasn't interested. He was assuming it was because of her past relationship.

Which was actually the truth. She was interested, and she'd said no because she was an idiot.

"It wasn't that recent and I'm not heartbroken. Maybe I just turned you down because I'm not attracted to you. Maybe you make me physically ill."

She couldn't help teasing him a little. He deserved it.

"Physically ill." He slapped a hand on his chest dramatically. "How painful. Is it my hideous face? My body? Or my boring personality? I know...I smell. That's it, isn't it?"

If only... Resisting him would be easy.

"All of those things," Sierra said matter-of-factly. "You're just not my type. But I guess you are Angela's type from what I've seen on set."

There. I said it.

He groaned and rolled his eyes. "She's a royal pain in the ass. I was warned about her but she's even worse than I thought."

"She spends a lot of time in your trailer," Sierra replied, holding her breath.

I am not jealous, though. It doesn't matter.

"I need a shoehorn to get rid of her," he scoffed. "Believe me, we're not doing what everyone thinks we're doing. Mostly she's driving me bat crap crazy."

"She is really beautiful."

"And crazy," Ryan added. "I'm not interested in her."

Sierra was happy to hear that but she wasn't quite ready to let this go.

"No one would blame you if you were."

"My friends would have me committed. I'm not interested. In her, anyway."

Ryan rolled closer so that she was looking into his blue eyes, their lips mere inches away from one another. If either of them moved even slightly, they would be kissing.

Move. Move closer. Kiss him.

She stayed as still as a statue. So did he.

But his gaze seemed to bore right through her, stripping her of all the veneer she'd built up to deal with the world over the years. It was as if he was seeing deep inside of her and that was scary.

"You, on the other hand, are a different matter," he said softly, his breath warm against her cheek. She quivered at the low timbre of his voice, so deep and dark when they were all alone like this. "You are definitely someone that I'm attracted to. And you smell amazing."

You do, too.

She didn't know how long they sat there and stared into one another's eyes. They were in their own little world tonight with the ice glistening all around them and the town tucked up into their own homes. She took in a lungful of his scent, her head spinning as it hit her veins. She could get lost in a man like this.

That's the one thing I'm not ready to do.

"Marshmallows."

Smiling, he sat back slightly. "Marshmallows?"

She swallowed hard, loath to end the moment but knowing she must. The pull toward him was strong and she could tell they both felt it. If she stayed here, something...physical was going to happen. "Yes, we should toast some marshmallows. You know, for dessert."

Before he could even reply she was standing, tugging her sweater down where it had rucked up. "I'll go get them. I'll be right back."

If he thought she was acting strangely, he didn't say it out loud.

"Do you need any help?"

Tons. It would be nice if you could be an asshole. I'm falling for you and this is a tad inconvenient.

"I've got it."

She turned and fled into the kitchen, but it was only a temporary respite. She couldn't run forever, and she wasn't sure she wanted to.

CHAPTER
Eleven

RYAN OPENED ONE EYE SLIGHTLY, shaking off the sleep that lay heavily on him. A gap in the drapes showed that it was still dark outside, although he didn't know exactly what time it was. Normally he'd be sleeping but a sound had woken him from his slumber in front of the fireplace.

He and Sierra had talked until almost midnight before making up a couple of beds - his on the floor and hers on the couch - near the fireplace and going to sleep. A glance at the empty sofa told him that what he'd heard had been Sierra. Sitting up, he looked around and saw her shadow in the kitchen moving about. Strangely, she hadn't taken the flashlight with her. If she wanted a drink or a snack, she was doing it in the dark. She must not want to wake him up, which was sweet.

Still dressed in sweatpants and a t-shirt, he stretched and stood, folding the blankets back. Despite the cold temperatures outside and the lack of electricity the small living room was pretty comfortable. The fire would need to be stoked up and more wood added but it was putting out a great deal of heat just from the simmering embers.

Padding on bare feet, he didn't try and be quiet. Scaring or surprising her was not on the agenda. It was better that she knew he was coming and this time he was going to bring a flashlight.

"Are you okay?"

Without shining the light in her eyes, he focused the beam close enough that her form was illuminated. She was down bent over, her legs together, touching her toes and then reaching as high up as she could go, before repeating the process.

Ryan heard a heavy sigh and then Sierra straightened, her hands laced behind her head in another stretch.

"I have a bad back and sometimes I can't sleep."

She was what...thirty or a little more? Far too young to have a bad back unless she had an injury. Maybe from sports or a job in the past.

"Did you hurt yourself? Do you have some sort of injury?"

There was silence and for a moment he thought she wasn't going to answer.

"Yes, I have an injury. I...spent some time in the hospital a few years ago. I have some lingering effects from then."

She didn't elaborate on how she'd been injured. It might have been a nasty car accident. One of his brothers had been hit from behind and to this day had a bad back and neck from it. He could tell when it was going to rain.

"Do you have some medicine for it? You know...an ointment? I could rub it on your back."

Now why did he say that? The words had jumped out of his mouth before he'd fully engaged his sleepy brain. He couldn't deny, however, the fact that he wanted to touch her and make her feel better. The thought of her in pain bothered him far more than it should.

Once again there was a long silence before she spoke.

"Yes, I have some of that stuff that goes cold. It's in the bedroom."

He had the flashlight. "If you tell me where it is, I can get it for you."

"No!" Her tone sounded distressed. "It's...in my night-stand drawer. I can get it."

Now his mind was wandering places it shouldn't go. Just what did this woman have in her nightstand drawer that she didn't want him to see? Toys? Condoms? Porn?

It's none of my business.

He held out the flashlight. "You'll need this. I'll wait by the fire. There's plenty of light in there without it."

She accepted it without a word and left the kitchen so he went back into the living room, stoking up the fire and adding another log. Chuckling, he wondered what he'd be doing at this moment if he hadn't smelled Sierra cooking dinner last night. Probably freezing his sorry ass off next door and trying not to fall asleep and die. Or maybe he would have come over anyway, found another excuse to see her.

That's what I would have done.

Pushing the blankets into a makeshift pallet she could lie on, he gave himself a stern talking to. This was only because she was in pain. She'd turned him down when he'd asked her out, although he could swear he saw an answering desire in her gaze. He wasn't a callow youth who didn't know shit about females. He was an experienced man who had been around the block a time or two. He could feel the mutual attraction as if it were a living thing but Sierra was running from it. He'd almost kissed her last night but his instincts had held him back.

She had to come to him. He wasn't the type to keep pushing or negotiating for what he wanted. He'd put it out there that he was attracted to her but the next move? She had to make it.

Ryan was so lost in thought that he hadn't heard her come back into the living room until she sat down on the floor next to him, shyly holding out a tube of a recognizable brand of gel for aches and pains. He'd used it himself a few times for sore muscles.

She looked nervous, her top teeth sinking down into her lush lower lip. "How do you want to do this?"

That's a loaded question. Any way you want to, honey.

Stay focused, man. Keep it together.

"Where all do you want this? Your upper back? Lower?"

She reached around and placed her hand on her lower spine. "Here and up on my shoulder blades too, if that's okay."

That was fine. The thought of getting to touch that much exposed flesh was exciting him like a schoolboy. He was acting like it had been months or years since he'd had sex. This was a simple act of kindness. Sierra was in pain and he had the means to aid it. This wasn't about his baser instincts.

At least, it shouldn't be.

Except that she totally looked adorable in her red plaid flannel pajama pants and black t-shirt. She was definitely not wearing a bra and despite the emanating heat from the fire her nipples poked against the cotton fabric, constantly drawing his attention. Her long hair was piled up in a messy bun on top of her head and it showed off the exquisite bone structure of her face. She wasn't wearing a smidgen of makeup but she was still incredibly gorgeous.

Frankly, he couldn't remember the last time he'd been in this intimate of a situation with a woman and the outcome hadn't been sex. There had been wine earlier, a roaring fire, blankets on the floor. Wasn't that the perfect recipe for wild lovemaking?

Jesus, I have sex on the brain. When did I become such a horndog?

"That's fine. Do you want to lie down on your stomach?"

Her eyes widened at his request but she did anyway, stretching out on the blankets he'd arranged for her comfort. He twisted off the top and was about to squirt a bunch into his palm but paused when he realized they still had one problem.

"You're going to have to lift your shirt." He cleared his throat and shifted slightly. "It would be easier if you took it off. I don't want to get this stuff on it. It might stain."

There was only a moment of hesitation and then she reached down and tugged her t-shirt up all the while still lying down, her front modestly turned away from him. She didn't toss it away, instead setting it right next to her as if to remind him that cover was only a fingertip away. *Don't try anything, buddy.*

He wouldn't dream of it. He'd meant it about her making the next move.

I'm not that hard up. I'm not the type to seduce an unwilling woman.

The gel was cold in his hand and he tried to warm it up between his fingers, but she still jumped slightly when he touched her skin. At first, he made long sweeping strokes up and down her back before concentrating on the spot between her shoulder blades that made her sigh and squirm.

Story boards for his next film. Baseball statistics. A Bolognese recipe that his mother had taught him. Ryan thought about anything and everything to keep from becoming aroused just stroking Sierra's beautifully soft skin. His fingers trailed up her sides, tickling her ribcage and she giggled, a sound that made his chest tight. He needed to keep his head on straight and not let a little bit of bare flesh make him crazy.

But oh, what bare flesh it was.

Creamy and soft, it glowed like pearls in the firelight. There was a freckle on one shoulder and another near the base of her spine. He had to resist an overwhelming urge to lean down and press his lips to it before trailing upward...or downward. At this point, he wasn't fussy. Her pajama pants had ridden lower on her hips and he could just spy the dimples at the top of her delightful bottom. He wouldn't mind kissing those, too.

His loose sweatpants had become increasingly uncomfortable and he should stop all of this madness. Right now. Pull his hands away from her tempting torso and put the cap back on his lust and this pain gel. Maybe standing outside in the ice and snow for a few hours would cool off his ardor.

But he simply wasn't going to do that. Because he was stupid and he didn't have a lick of common sense. Defiantly, he squeezed more gel onto his palm. Like his dad always used to say...

If a job is worth doing, it's worth doing well.

CHAPTER
Twelve

SIERRA WAS GOING SLOWLY, excruciatingly insane. Ryan's touch was incredibly gentle, yet sensual at the same time. It had been a long time for her...too long if her sizzling reaction was anything to go by. With barely a brush of his fingers, she'd gone up in flames. She'd long ago forgotten any pain or discomfort in her back but she wouldn't budge from this spot for anything. It felt too wondrous and amazing.

That tension that had been building between them all night was so thick it was like a stack of bricks pushing her into the blankets, keeping her from stopping him. Not that she wanted to. If she had her way, this would go on forever and ever. It was like floating on a cloud of pleasure and no one came down from Cloud Nine voluntarily.

Get a hold of yourself.

Nope, don't think I will. This feels far too good and I don't want to stop.

I want this and there's no good reason not to have it. And him.

Billie's words were echoing in Sierra's brain. *Have fun. Enjoy yourself. You deserve this.*

All the reasons she should just go for it. The only thing holding her back was her own self-doubt. Ryan had made it clear he wanted her, she could see it in his eyes. He was also aware that she returned those feelings. She was terrible at hiding the attraction.

The tension had been simmering between them all night and this had really been inevitable, if she were honest with herself. She'd known it when she'd invited him to stay with her. She could say she simply didn't want him to freeze to death but deep inside she'd known what it meant. Their crazy back and forth flirtation was about to come to an end. They were going to take the next scary - for her, at least - step. He might be far out of her league but right now she wanted him so much she didn't care.

You set the ground rules, then he won't know you don't know the game.

Lifting up slightly, Sierra reached for her shirt and slid it under her, holding it over her breasts. She needed every ounce of bravery at this point to go so far out of her comfort zone. Feeling her movement, he'd paused as she turned over. For some reason, it was important to see his expression, the look in his eyes.

"Feel better?"

She did but it was only partly from the gel he'd rubbed so carefully and gently into her sore back.

"Yes," she said, automatically nodding. "I–I think we need to talk."

His lips twisted and he sucked in a sharp breath. "Believe me, I'm not trying to pressure you, honey. I swear. I get it. You said no and that's it. I can accept rejection. I may not like it but I can take it."

If she didn't do it now, she'd chicken out and always wonder what might have been. With every ounce of courage she possessed she sat up and cupped his stubbled cheek with the palm of her hand.

"Ryan, I'm not saying no. I'm saying yes."

———

Ryan didn't move at first, seemingly stunned by her admission. He stared for a long moment and then a smile spread across his too handsome face. Her own heart lurched in her chest and the breath she'd been holding blew out slowly. Despite her inexperience, she hadn't been reading the situation wrong.

That had been a real fear in the back of her head. That she'd imagined all this sexual tension between them and if she made a move he'd be confused. Then he'd have to let her down gently and that would be a nightmare. How on earth could she possible finish the movie and see him every day when she was mortified to her very bones?

His fingers brushed up her arm and curled around the back of her neck. For a moment she tensed, memories of not-so-gentle touches flooding her brain but then she reminded herself that this was Ryan. This wasn't her evil ex-husband. She relaxed against his hand, enjoying the tingle that flesh on flesh brought. This was what she'd craved. Two people touching, wanting to bring the other pleasure. She barely remembered it.

"Are you sure?" He looked happy but conflicted. "Baby, I really like you and believe me, I want to make love to you but you have to know that I'm–"

She placed her own fingers over his lips. "It's okay. I'm not looking for a commitment. I'm definitely not looking for a husband."

That was literally the last thing she wanted.

His shoulders sagged in relief but there was still hesitation in his eyes. "It's just my work takes me all over the world–"

"I mean it, Ryan. I get it. We both have busy careers. I'm not trying to make this something it's not. We're both adults here and we both know not everything leads to forever."

She hadn't thought it would be this difficult to convince him. In her experience, a man would just go for it when given the green light. Or even a yellow one.

There was honesty in his gaze, but there was fear, too. He might be thinking that she would pull away if he spoke too much of the truth.

"I just don't want there to be any misunderstandings," he said, his voice hoarse and tortured. "I can't offer you anything past this ice storm and that sounds really piss poor. I wouldn't blame you if you threw me out in the cold. You deserve better."

That made her smile. He didn't get it at all. "What is it with all men that you think women are only after one thing - a husband? I'm not. I'm not looking for commitment. I've had that and frankly, it wasn't all it was cracked up to be. What I'm looking for now is some no-strings fun. Just some time to enjoy myself while the power's out and it's freezing. There's no one here but you and me, Ryan. This can just be for us. No one else."

This is no time to be nervous or scared. Go for it. This is your chance.

She didn't know if she'd convinced him but if she hadn't he didn't seem to care any longer, groaning deep in his chest and capturing her lips with his own. They fell back on the cushions together, his hands immediately tugging away the shirt she'd used to cover her bare breasts. At the same time, her own impatient fingers were pulling his t-shirt from the waistband of his sweatpants. She couldn't wait to feel every inch of his flesh pressed to every inch of her own.

His tongue swiped at her lower lip, gaining access to her mouth. His kiss was playful but demanding. He wasn't content for her to play a passive role as she was used to. He wanted her to be a full participant and she reveled in the opportunity to return each kiss and caress with one or two of her own.

Kicking his pants away, he was totally naked to her gaze and she feasted on the perfect specimen of male beauty in front of her. Muscular but not overly so, he had a body more like a swimmer than a body builder. Wide shoulders, ridged abs, and powerful thighs. His skin glowed golden in the firelight and she couldn't stop herself from reaching out and running her fingers down his torso, drawing a moan from his lips.

She hadn't realized how sexy it could be listening to a man moan and groan from pleasure she was giving him but it was a heady concoction. It made her even bolder and she allowed her fingertips to wander all over his chest and shoulders before meandering down the silky treasure trail low on his belly.

She wanted to wrap her hand around him, measure with her fingers to be sure her eyes weren't deceiving her. He was long, hard, and thick, and as a woman who had only seen two cocks in her entire life he seemed far too large to be real. It was a little intimidating but beautiful all at the same time.

"Baby," he rasped as her fingernail traced a blue vein down the side of his cock. It jumped when she touched it, drawing a giggle from her lips. "You're killing me here."

Sierra looked up and frowned. "Do you want me to stop?"

"Fuck, no."

Then she was confused. "What do you want me to do?"

"Take me in your mouth, baby. I need to feel it."

Ah, oral sex. She wasn't exactly a rookie but it was something she had spent a great deal of time avoiding. Eventually Brian had stopped trying to make her do it, content to simply pump in and out of her to get his own. He'd never cared much about her, if at all. He'd once said that women having orgasms was a sin, and that sex wasn't for them. It was for men. She hadn't believed it but she'd sure realized pretty early that there weren't going to be many orgasms with Brian. Now Ryan...that was a whole different story. He wouldn't take and not give. Would he?

Trusting that he wouldn't be selfish, she leaned down and ran her tongue along the same path her fingertips had just traveled. His body arched up off of the cushions and she could hear his teeth snap together. She must be on the right track if he reacted like that. The feeling of euphoria and power came over her again and she drew him slowly into her mouth as far as she could take him, swirling her tongue as she did so. His breath came out in a hiss and a spark ran down her own spine. This was fun, experimenting as to how he would react when she did this or that.

She pulled almost all the way off of his cock before plunging it back into her mouth, bumping the back of her throat. Over and over she repeated the motion, keeping her lips tight until he was panting underneath her. His fingers were tangled in her hair at the back of her head, thrusting into her mouth but abruptly he pulled back until her mouth slid off with a pop.

"If you keep doing that, this is going to be all over fast. You are far too good at that, baby. You could make a man lose his mind."

For a moment she didn't get what he was saying but his meaning finally sunk into her muddled brain. He wanted to make this last. Honestly, so did she.

And I did good. He loved it.

Apparently, enthusiasm could indeed make up for lack of experience and skill.

He levered up to a sitting position and kissed her swollen lips, playing a game of keep-away with his tongue before finally pulling back. Their foreheads rested against each other and their breathing was ragged. Technically, they hadn't even had sex yet and this was about the most aroused she'd ever been. A coil had already begun tightening low in her belly and that little voice in her head was urging her on. Relax, cut loose, enjoy this moment. She intended to do just that.

He nudged her backward onto the blankets and cushions. "I think you need a little attention. I want to worship this beautiful body."

Who am I to say no?

CHAPTER
Thirteen

SIERRA SIMPLY TOOK Ryan's breath away. Her straightforward honesty, her innate generosity, and the passion that he'd only guessed at but was clearly burning in her eyes. She'd gone up in flames at his touch and his own flesh burned, white hot with need. Even now as she lay in the glow from the fireplace she was so fucking gorgeous he had to hold himself back from falling on her like a starving dog with a bone.

The air was heady with the perfume of their arousal mixed with a touch of sweat. Their skin was damp from their exertions despite the temperature outside. The room felt hot but it had nothing to do with the blazing fire only a few feet away. It was all Sierra.

His gaze caressed her head to toe, lingering on her creamy breasts with their rose-tipped nipples. Just the right size for his hands. Moving farther down, he slowed at the soft curve of her hip before traveling the length of her legs all the way to her red painted toes. He was already imagining those long limbs wrapped around his waist as he thrust them both to heaven. His lower back ached and his balls were pulled up tight, but patience would make their final explosion far better and sweeter.

First...he had plans. All of them included hearing her call his name when she came. More than once.

Leaning over her, he dipped his head down to take a pebbled nipple into his mouth, worrying it between his lips and scraping it gently with his teeth. Her hands flew to the back of his head as her body bowed. Beautiful. Nothing was more sensuous than seeing Sierra with her eyes closed, her head thrown back, and her lips parted in a moan. So fucking sexy. This woman played him so easily.

Ryan moved to the neglected breast, drawing more sounds from the back of Sierra's throat. If she was trying to say something he didn't understand a word but her hands anchored at the back of his head clearly told him...

Don't stop.

Nuzzling between her breasts, he placed open-mouthed kisses all the way down her torso, stopping to run his tongue in her belly button before continuing the damp path to the place he most wanted to be. Right between her thighs.

"Open for me, baby. I want to hear you scream my name when you come."

He nudged her legs apart, his tongue running along the seam of her thigh where it met her hip. She bucked underneath him, a gasp escaping from between her lips but he placed tiny baby kisses on her inner thigh until she was still again, although her entire body trembled in response.

The first touch of his tongue on her clit had her nails

digging into his scalp. She mewled as his tongue traced her folds and then circled her clit, never quite giving her what she needed to go over. Teasing and building the pleasure, layering it, was half the fun. She was moving restlessly under him, saying his name softly under her breath when he pressed first one and then a second finger inside of her.

Christ, she was snug. Fucking this woman was going to be pure, unadulterated bliss.

And short if he wasn't careful.

Crooking his fingers in a come-hither motion to rub that sweet spot inside of her, he closed his mouth over her swollen pearl and gently sucked. Because he'd taken her to the precipice, she fell over instantly at his intimate touch. This time she did cry out his name as her walls tightened on his fingers, almost drawing them farther in.

He drew out her climax as long as he could before climbing up her body and pressing a kiss to the spot where her pulse beat madly at the base of her throat.

"Are you ready for me, baby?"

She nodded, still breathless from her orgasm and her hands traveled down to his ass, giving him an encouraging squeeze. Positioning himself between her thighs, he nudged her entrance and then froze, reality smacking him in the face. Thank God his brain wasn't completely devoid of blood.

"Sierra," he groaned. "We need protection. I have some next door."

Her eyes widened and then his words seemed to make sense. She took a deep breath, her cheeks turning red. "I have some here."

That was the best damn news he'd heard in a long time.

He hadn't wanted to go out into the cold but he wanted her so badly he would have and gladly. But this was much better.

But she was still talking, a little fast and nervously.

"My sister put them in my cosmetics bag. I wasn't planning on...you know...this. She just wanted me to be prepared...just in case."

For some reason, Sierra was embarrassed to have condoms. She didn't need to be. He was thrilled that she was responsible enough to be prepared.

"Tell me where they are and I'll go get them. You stay here and keep warm."

Her legs might be a little wobbly after her climax, although it wasn't exactly easy for him to walk with a huge hard on. She explained where her travel cosmetics case was located and he took the flashlight and quickly retrieved the box. A twelve-pack. That might just be enough depending on how long the power stayed out.

When he returned to the living room, she held out her arms and he tossed away the flashlight on the couch and knelt down close. She had the softest skin and he could spend all day running his hands over it, delighting in the difference between their bodies. Hers so soft and curved and inviting.

After. I can do that afterward.

Giggling like teenagers, they fumbled with opening the box and then the foil packet. It should have felt strange and awkward but it was nice, this friendliness mixed with desire. Laughing with a lover was almost as good as climaxing with one. This wasn't something he was used to but he liked it. Even if they hadn't made love, he genuinely enjoyed Sierra's company.

Rolling on the condom, he didn't hover above her like last time, instead lying down beside her and rolling her onto her side so he was spooning her back. He lifted her top leg up and back and rested it on his before beginning to push inside of her welcoming channel. Her muscles gripped him, guiding his way and pulling him deeper.

He buried his face in the crook of her neck, her scent teasing his nostrils as he breathed in deeply. His chest tightened painfully as he watched the pleasure on her face as he withdrew slightly and then thrust back in. Her sighs were music to his needy ears.

One arm slid underneath Sierra to pluck at a hard nipple while the other hand slid down her belly to the warm and damp juncture of her thighs. His fingers brushed her clit, making circles around it as he lazily thrust in and out, determined to take his time. He wanted to watch her come again almost as much as he wanted to himself. The pressure in his lower back was becoming unbearable but he gritted his teeth and ignored it. Nothing was going to rush him.

Except her. She was moving now, pushing herself back every time he pushed forward. Her breath came in pants and moans, her movements more frenzied as she neared her peak. Her nails dug into his arm and she whispered his name like an incantation, casting a spell over the two of them as if they were the only lovers left on the planet. The storm had created this amazingly private moment, the entire world hidden under a blanket of ice. It would melt

eventually but for now it shielded them from the cold real-
ities outside of these walls.

"Now, Ryan," she breathed. "Harder. Faster."

Picking up the pace, he pistoned in and out of her,
blood pumping loudly in his ears. He groaned loudly as
his orgasm hit him sideways like a freight train, starting at
his spine and pulling him inside out. He squeezed his eyes
shut but then pried them open again to watch Sierra fall.
He wanted to see her beautiful face at that particular
moment.

Her climax quickly followed, his fingers speeding up as
he rubbed her sensitive button until she exploded. She did
call his name again and her head fell back onto his damp
chest, her expression one of total bliss.

Their bodies went limp, their skin sticky from sweat.
He didn't bother to move and he couldn't have even if he
wanted to. She'd worn him out, at least for now, but he
was going to want her again. His hunger was building
already. She reached out and softly stroked the rapidly
cooling flesh of his arm.

"That was...amazing."

Her warm breath huffed against his shoulder, sending a
shudder of pleasure through him. Everything she did felt
good.

He chuckled and nuzzled her cheek. "It was. We should
do it again when we're rested up."

"I think I'd like that."

For now, he'd happily stay under the spell. He'd worry
about tomorrow...later.

CHAPTER
Fourteen

IT SHOULD HAVE FELT strange to wake up in Ryan's arms but it didn't. If anything, it felt wonderful and definitely worth repeating. She'd woken before him and had spent the time simply enjoying being held. Her marriage hadn't included physical affection except maybe at the beginning, but that had always been to get sex. No one had ever held her just because it felt nice. Not her mother, not the few boyfriends she'd had, and certainly not her loser of a husband.

He smelled good, too. She breathed his scent in deeply while letting her gaze run all over his face and body. He was a handsome man, although not a pretty boy. Now that she had the time to inspect him, she could see that his nose was slightly crooked and his eyebrow had a tiny scar right at the corner. It made him even more endearing as she pictured him as a little boy falling off his bicycle or maybe sliding into third base during a Little League game. All those normal childhood activities she'd only seen on television but had never experienced herself.

She was so lost in thought that she didn't notice that one of his eyes had opened and a smile had curled his lips.

"Do I pass, honey?"

Jerking her gaze back to his face, she could feel the warmth invading her cheeks. So busted.

"Pass?"

"Inspection." He stretched lazily, the blanket falling down around his lean waist as he sat up. "You seemed to be looking at me as if you were trying to decide if I passed inspection. Do I?"

Oh hell yes.

"For the most part." She gave him her best flirtatious smile, although playfulness with a man wasn't something she excelled at. All she could think about was if she had dragon breath and Medusa hair. "Did you sleep okay?'

She didn't know what else to ask or say. How did one make small talk the morning after? Should she offer to make breakfast? Just what was the protocol?

Make your own rules.

Billie's words echoed in her head, reminding her that Sierra didn't have to follow a script. She could do whatever she wanted to. She'd probably never see Ryan again unless it was at some fancy Hollywood party and that would be from across the room. By then they would have both moved on.

Or at least he would have.

He leaned down and dropped a brief but firm kiss on her lips. If she had dragon breath, he at least didn't faint.

"Best damn night's sleep I've had since I started this movie. Hmmm...I wonder why? What could be different?"

The flush that had started in her cheeks grew and she could feel the heat all the way to her chest and ears.

"I slept good, too."

His smile fell and his brows pulled down. "Are you sure? You were in some pain earlier. How's your back now? We didn't hurt it more when we... I tried to pick a position that wouldn't make it worse."

His voice trailed off but she understood what he was saying. That he'd been so kind to think of her comfort and well-being at such an intimate moment was simply another point in his favor. He appeared to be a genuinely good person.

If I can trust my instincts. I've made mistakes in the past.

"It's fine," she said quickly, her hand flying to that spot that usually ached right above her left hip. "Much better."

Although she wouldn't mind more of that pain gel. The rush of endorphins from the orgasm had helped a whole lot, too.

"We'll put some more gel on this morning," he promised, levering up to stoke the fire and add some wood. Completely unconcerned about his nudity, the blanket fell away exposing his firm buttocks and his muscled thighs. Such a beautiful man. "How did you hurt your back? Car accident? You don't look the type to play rugby or football."

It was meant as a joke and if she was smart she'd smile and laugh at it, then make some joke about sky diving and extreme cliff diving. They'd both giggle and she could change the subject.

But...there was a part deep inside of her that was tired of lying, because that's what it was. It might be lying by omission but it was still lying. Her past was a part of her life and with a hell of a lot of help from Billie, Tyler, and her therapist, she was coming to grips with it. That meant being honest about it. What happened to her wasn't her fault. It was Brian's fault.

They could argue all day about how long she'd stayed but her self-esteem had been battered too and she simply hadn't thought she was worth having any other life. Not until that night she'd lain there on the kitchen floor thinking she was dying. It was then that she'd found the will to have a different and better life. She'd found that strength to call the police and this time press charges, telling the cop she wanted him in jail. There had been no wavering when the social worker had come into her hospital room, the same one she'd seen the two times before that.

Sierra wanted out. She wanted a better life and she wanted Brian to pay for what he'd done. And she sure as hell didn't want any other woman to go through this, too. He needed to learn that hitting a woman wasn't the answer to his problems.

If Ryan thought any less of her because she'd been a battered woman then...well...she'd have to live with that. There would always be people who were going to judge her.

"No, it wasn't a car accident," she heard herself reply. She could have stopped there but she didn't. It was time to stand up to Brian in this final way. She'd left this one chain on for too long. He didn't get to control her romantic relationships, too. Not now, not ever. The proverbial key had always been in her hand and now was the time to use it to open the locks. "My ex-husband abused me and I ended up in the hospital several times. The last time was the worst and that's when I moved out to California with Billie and Tyler and divorced him."

That was an edited version, without all the dirty details, but no one needed to know just how pathetic she'd been at that low point in her life. Literally the lowest point ever.

Ryan's mouth fell open and his eyes widened before he gained control over his expression. Clearly, she'd shocked him, though.

His mouth then snapped shut and a muscle worked in his jaw. "Please tell me the son of a bitch is in jail. Or six feet under."

"He was in jail but now he's not. He is on probation and is not allowed anywhere near me."

Growling, Ryan bared his teeth. "A restraining order? A bunch of words not worth the piece of paper they're printed on. You need round the clock security. I can arrange–"

Holding up her hand, Sierra shook her head. It was sweet that he was all protective but he didn't need to go off the deep end. It had been handled.

"Hold on. It's lovely that you feel that way but he's not going to come anywhere near me. If he does, he goes back to jail. That's the deal he made with the courts. Add in the fact that he can't hold down a job, he couldn't put the money together to travel to California or anywhere that I'm filming." Then she said out loud what she'd only suspected. "Besides, I'm pretty sure that Tyler paid him off. I've never asked him and he's never said anything but he came home one day and basically told me I didn't have anything to fear ever again."

"Paid him off?" Ryan scoffed. "I would have *scared* him off. Maybe a few broken bones might have cleared up his confusion as to how to treat a woman."

"Tyler and his friends wanted to do that but Billie and I put a stop to that immediately. Can you imagine the press? No, this was better. He's never tried to contact me since I left so I think he's done and moved on. The only thing I worry about is him talking to the press or something equally humiliating, but I'm guessing Tyler took care of that as well."

"What a low life piece of scum. I'd like just five minutes in a room alone with him."

That made Sierra laugh and he looked shocked when she did. "You'd have to wait in line behind Tyler, Sam, Nate, Max, and my sister Billie, who might just fight dirtier than all of them put together. I doubt there'd be much left of him by the time you got your turn."

He shook his head, his expression puzzled. "Aren't you angry? Don't you want revenge?"

Sierra was no saint. She'd often thought about many scenarios in which Brian was paid back in spades for his behavior. But she'd also learned that being the one to dish it out wasn't going to be as satisfying as she imagined. It was best to let karma sort him out.

"Wanting revenge leaves me tied to him," she explained. "It means he still has power over me and that's something he's never going to have again. He doesn't get to mess with my emotions or my happiness anymore. I've blessed and released the mistakes I made in the past and I'm moving forward with my life. I just don't want to be angry. His life sucks and frankly, I don't feel badly about that. My decisions might not have been the best but his were far worse. He's reaping what he sowed, and I don't want to give him any more space in my head. He won't live there rent free."

"You didn't make any mistakes, he did."

She studied his features, looking for even a sign of disdain but seeing none. How about that?

"Many people would judge me for not leaving earlier, for staying. It was only when I thought I was dying that I found the strength to leave." She took a deep breath, admitting it was almost physically painful. Her chest felt too tight for her body. "I was to the point that I didn't think I was worth anything. Self-esteem? I had none. I was convinced that what he did was all my fault. That I brought it on myself."

He seemed to digest her words, his gaze skittering away before coming back to rest on her face. "And the first time it happened?"

She remembered it well. Too well.

"He cried and said he was sorry. He said it would never happen again. I wanted to be loved so badly after my shitty childhood that I believed him. I gave him a second chance."

"What did he do to you? That last time?" The question came out low, Ryan's voice barely audible. "How did he hurt you?"

Easy question. She knew her medical records like the back of her hand.

"Broken arm, concussion, twisted neck and back, tons of bruises and cuts. I had a nasty black eye but at least that last time he didn't break my nose." She touched the bridge of her nose. "Billie and Tyler paid for the surgery to repair it. I could barely breathe through it and I snored like a freight train."

Then she reached around to the back of her head, underneath her hair. "I have a permanent bald spot back here where he dragged me by my hair once. It won't grow back but it's small and my hair is thick so it's no big deal."

"Scars?"

Ryan sounded like someone had punched him in the gut and then did an upper cut to the throat. He certainly wasn't going to go easy on himself and by God it felt good to tell someone. Sure, Billie, Tyler, and her therapist knew, but this was different. It really was throwing off those final shackles.

"I have a few but he was careful most of the time to hit me where it wouldn't show. It was only toward the end that he got sloppy."

His hands were clenched into fists, the knuckles white. "Now I want to kill him more than ever. That he hurt you like that–"

He broke off, clearing his throat several times before continuing. "He's not a man, someone like him. He's worse than an animal. He better hope he never comes near you because I will wait in line and take my turn."

She didn't need him to fight her battles but it felt

wonderful that he wanted to. She had friends and family now. She wasn't alone.

"He isn't worth it," she replied simply. "He's a waste of skin. Billie said that he ought to apologize to the trees that are working tirelessly to provide him with clean oxygen to breathe. His life sucks and he wastes every day of that precious gift being a total jerk to everyone around him."

"It's not justice," Ryan growled. "He should be in prison."

"That's not how the system works and I had to make peace with that a long time ago. I suggest you do the same."

He shook his head, the frown back on his face. "How can you be so calm? So...forgiving?"

He didn't understand but then most didn't. "I don't forgive him. But I forgave myself, Ryan. I want to be happy. I want to have fun and live my life to its fullest. I almost didn't get to do that. Holding on to anger and pain just chips away at the joy in myself. But I didn't get here on my own, I had a lot of help. I've been in therapy and that's made a huge difference."

"That's good." Ryan shrugged awkwardly. "I don't know much about therapy. How did it help you?"

"I'm not ashamed anymore."

"You have nothing to be ashamed of," he said quickly. "Not a thing."

I didn't always know that.

"I know. That's why I told you." She'd done the right thing, telling him. A weight was lifted from her shoulders and she felt lighter somehow. She didn't have to tell everyone she met about her past and honestly, she didn't plan to, but she didn't have to pretend either when she allowed someone into her circle of friends. "Now how about we wrangle up some breakfast? I bet you're starving."

Time to put the past away. She'd told him and now she wanted to simply live her life. And until the lights came back on, she was content to live it with Ryan.

CHAPTER
Fifteen

RYAN WAS a workaholic and rarely took any downtime for himself but if he could sit in this hot bathtub with Sierra more often he might be persuaded. He'd been shocked and delighted when Sierra had told him that the water heater ran off of natural gas. They might not have heat but they had hot water. Of course, he probably still would have frozen to death all alone next door because he would have been too stupid to check.

His fingers trailed down her damp arm and then her thigh, the skin satin soft but the muscles underneath firm and taut. It was such a contradiction and it fascinated him, making him want to explore every inch of her body here in this candlelit bathroom. It was frustrating that he couldn't get a good look at her in the bright light of day.

"I've told you my life story," she murmured, cuddling deeper into his arms. Neither one of them wanted to get out of the warm tub. The air was freezing this far away from the fireplace. "I want to hear more about your life. Do you like being a director?"

"I love it. I was a lousy actor, something you'll realize if you watch any of those movies."

"I don't believe that for a minute. I bet you were a great actor."

He shook his head, remembering back when he first went to Hollywood. "No, I sucked. Really badly. I couldn't seem to get out of my own head and into the character's. I was always looking around at the other actors and what was happening technically."

A delicately arched brow rose. "I'm definitely going to rent those films. They can't possibly be as bad as you say."

"Nothing good can come from that," he warned with a chuckle. "Besides, you'd have to watch an entire two-hour film to see me for ten minutes. I wasn't actually Jack Nicholson."

She turned back around with a sigh, and again rested her head on his chest. "Is that your idol?"

"He's one of them. I like Pacino and DeNiro too."

"Everyone likes Pacino and DeNiro."

That was true. It was almost a cliché.

"What about you? Are you a Meryl Streep fan?"

"Of course. She was amazing in *The Devil Wears Prada*, but we're not talking about me. We're talking about you."

"I liked that movie, too."

He was just playing with her and he got a dig in the ribs with her elbow as a reply. Damn, she had pointy elbows.

"So what else do you want to do? You've won an Oscar. That's pretty much the pinnacle of this business, right?"

His laughter dislodged her head, which made her scowl up at him. "Are you saying that I've peaked, babe, and it's only downhill from here? Jesus, I hope not. I have big plans for the future."

"Okay, now we're getting somewhere. What are these big plans?"

He'd never told a single soul about all the items on his crazy director bucket list, but she'd revealed her painful past honestly, so it felt like he should admit to his own somewhat insane future. Not that anything on the list was sure to happen. It was a list and so far he'd been able to mark off several items but there were so many more. He'd have to live to be a hundred and ten to do them all. And that was just his career list. His personal bucket list was completely different. Sadly, he'd only marked a few off of that one. Too busy working.

"The main one is that I want to make a movie in every country on the planet." That didn't come out right. "Wait, that's not exactly right. I want to film in every country but it can be for multiple movies."

She didn't laugh which was a point in her favor. "So a scene in Paris, and another in Rome? That sounds like fun but exhausting."

"Anything worth doing is going to be work. At least that's what my dad told me when I was a lazy-ass teenager and didn't want to mow the lawn."

"What else did he tell you?"

That question made Ryan laugh again. His father's advice had usually turned out to be excellent but as a youth it hadn't always been understood or appreciated.

"He told me that I shouldn't work too hard to figure out women. It was more fun for them to be a mystery."

"Was he right?"

"At the time I thought he was crazy," Ryan remembered, a grin on his face. "But I think that he was on to something there. Just enjoy the ride, so to speak. Men and women are different and there's no reason to bang my head against the wall trying to figure out why."

Her soft giggle made his heart squeeze in his chest. He liked her far too much.

"What other advice did he have?"

"Work hard whether I get rewarded or not. Always be the first one in to work and the last to leave. I still do that when I'm making a picture. Respect women and don't make them cry. Buy them flowers. Take a shower and don't be the smelly kid in school. That's one of my favorites."

"Words to live by," Sierra said solemnly but her lips were twitching with mirth. "Your father was a wise man. Did he ever give any advice about shoes?"

He didn't think she was serious but Ryan searched his mind anyway. It would be funny if the family patriarch had given him such advice.

"I can't think of any but he was a loafers kind of guy with bare feet on the weekends. He used to take me to the beach all of the time. He was a surfer and he taught me, too. He taught all of us actually."

"Did your mom go, too?"

"Sometimes. She was really good but I think she enjoyed the peace and quiet of the house when we were all out of it. Later when we got to be teenagers she went with us all of the time. I think because she didn't see us as much."

Ryan wasn't sure if it was a good idea to discuss his happy family life with Sierra. She'd never experienced anything like that and he didn't want her to feel...badly. He didn't want to bring up crappy memories of the past.

She didn't seem bothered, however, a smile curving her full lips. Lips made for kissing and doing other naughty stuff. His cock stirred to life at the thought of what they'd been doing just prior to taking this bath.

Twisting around, Sierra stared up at him in shock. "Are you kidding? You're getting a stiffie from thinking about surfing?"

Laughter bubbled from his lips at her outrage. This woman was completely adorable. She made him crack up at the strangest things.

"No, babe. I was actually pondering the dirty things we were doing to one another before we got in the tub. It wasn't surfing, although I love it. I just don't love it that much."

"Oh. That was kind of fun."

He pretended to be hurt, his lower lip sticking out. "Only kind of? I'm wounded."

She turned so that she was on her knees between his legs, facing him. Her hands ran down his torso, lingering on the quivering muscles of his abs. "Wounded, huh? Where? I'll kiss it better."

There was merriment in her expression, a devilish gleam that always turned out well for him. If she wanted to play games, he'd happily join in.

"Right about where your hands are...actually a little lower."

"If I kiss that spot better, I'll drown. Maybe we should get out of the tub and take this search mission back to the fireplace."

The water was cooling off.

Ryan heaved himself out of the tub, his arousal impossible to hide. If she didn't know how much he wanted her before, she did now.

"Let me get a towel and I'll dry you off." He pointed to his cock. "Just so we're clear, the spot is right here."

Sierra's kiss would make it all better.

———

When the lights came on hours later, both Sierra and Ryan were dozing in front of the fire, exhausted from a day of sex, fun, and junk food. They'd read to each other, they'd played strip poker, they'd even stuck their heads out of the house for a few minutes to see the ice beginning to melt. The temperature had risen steadily all day and by mid-afternoon was in the comfortable mid-forties.

Clearly, she hadn't thought ahead because everything that she had on when the power went out came back to life all at once. Loud and bright. The lamps clicked on along with the kitchen light, and the blast of sound from the television had them both practically jumping from their warm nest of blankets.

Ryan rubbed at his face, still groggy. "I guess the power is back on."

It was an obvious statement but they were a little out of

it. She pushed her hair out of her eyes and groaned. "I guess it is. I better check the thermostat. I turned it up before the ice storm to get the house good and toasty in case the power went out."

"Might as well leave it for a little while," Ryan replied, levering up and stretching, the covers falling around his waist to reveal bare skin that she had thoroughly explored earlier. "It'll warm up faster. You can turn it down later."

She was already standing, a blanket wrapped around her naked body. "I want to check everything anyway. I'll be right back."

First job was to turn the television to the local news, which was all video of the town covered in ice and cars sliding off of the road and into ditches. According to the annoyingly perky reporter, about fifty percent of the town still didn't have power but most should by morning. The more rural areas would take longer.

Sierra fussed with the thermostat and then went into the kitchen. The refrigerator was humming and that was good news. She'd have to toss pretty much everything but luckily she didn't keep much food in the house. Grabbing two bottles of water, she rejoined Ryan in the living room. He'd put on his sweat pants and stoked up the fire.

He was halfway to dressed. Their interlude was over. The temperature had risen, the ice was melting, and the power was back on. Reality had returned and their own little world was disappearing at a rapid rate.

It was never real. It was only a momentary fantasy.

"Anything interesting on the news?"

He turned at the sound of her voice. "Just a lot of people out driving that shouldn't be. I'm a California boy but even I know that you can't operate a motor vehicle on a sheet of ice."

The news was showing a car sliding into a parked truck on a residential street, then the car did a one-eighty and took out a mailbox and a garden gnome.

"I just like to think that people are overly optimistic and not stupid."

He dragged his t-shirt over his head. "You may be the nicest person I've ever met, but you have a point. I read once that something like ninety percent of the population thinks they're an above average driver. Statistically that's impossible. Ninety is greater than fifty."

"Are you an above average driver?"

His grin told the story. "Hell, yes."

Sierra wasn't sure what to do now. Ryan had redressed and she was standing around wearing a blanket. Was he going to leave? Did he want to leave? She'd assumed that he'd be around for dinner but now that the lights were on, she wasn't sure.

She inched backward slowly toward the bedroom. "I think I'll go get dressed. Now that the power is back on, I was thinking about making some macaroni and cheese for dinner. You're welcome to stay if you want. Or whatever."

He frowned but nodded. "I'd like that."

She would, too. They'd make their little world last a few hours longer and pretend that reality wasn't storming the gate.

It was lovely while it lasted.

CHAPTER
Sixteen

SIERRA WAS JUMPY, nervous and generally distracted. Every now and then while they'd cooked dinner, he'd watched her go off somewhere. Her thoughts were far from this cozy kitchen and the smell of melted cheese. He'd poured them some wine, hoping the alcohol would relax her but she'd barely touched it as they'd eaten dinner. They were both hungry, so conversation had lagged but their plates were clean and their stomachs full. She still hadn't said much but he could feel the tension and energy pouring off of her. She was practically vibrating in her chair.

She picked up her wine glass but didn't take a drink, slapping it back on the table.

"So I guess I'll just be up front and ask. How do we do this tomorrow? Do we pretend we barely know each other? Do we act like good friends? I'm not familiar with how this works the next day."

That's why she'd been acting so strangely. It wasn't a

bad question, either. They'd promised no recriminations, no regrets. Have a fun, sexy affair and then move on with their lives but they hadn't really talked about how to do that. Already he was thinking that he didn't really want it to end. They had another week to ten days of shooting and he wouldn't mind spending as much time as he could in bed with Sierra.

Bad idea. She's the kind of woman you get serious about. Don't go there, dude.

Ryan wasn't in any position to make any promises. His career was too demanding and he wasn't even sure if he wanted to be tied down to one woman.

He was pretty sure he didn't.

This also wasn't his first casual affair but it was Sierra's. Of course, she was going to be feeling a little unsure as to the next steps. He wanted to reassure her that he wasn't going to turn into an asshole. They would still be friends. Good friends.

"I'm not going to pretend not to know you," he replied after a long pause. "We'll just act naturally, like we did before. We're friends."

Her smile was sad. "Not really. If there's one thing I've learned in my short time in the movie business is that a person rarely stays friends with those they've met on set. You come together to do this huge project, and you get incredibly close to people, and then you all go your separate ways when it's over. It's strange but I'm getting used to it."

Sierra was right. Sure, there were a few people he'd clicked with and had stayed close with over the years but for the most part everyone moved on to the next movie without a backward glance. It didn't make them bad people, it was simply the nature of the beast. Making a film was an all-encompassing activity. It took all of his time, attention, and passion. It didn't leave much of anything for others.

"It doesn't make us less than friends right now," he argued. "Just because we won't text each other every five minutes doesn't mean that this doesn't matter. I just don't do relationships very well. I'm not good at compromise, and if I'm honest, I don't think I've ever compromised for any woman."

She was silent but she nodded as if she agreed.

"So we're buddies...pals? But we don't ask each other for compromises? Okay."

"If you were in trouble and needed help, you could call me. I'd be there."

Her brows rose and she didn't look convinced.

"I mean it. If you were arrested and thrown in a Turkish prison I'd pull every string I know to try and get you out. I'd probably fail but I'd try."

He'd made her laugh, which was a relief. This conversation had become far too serious.

"A Turkish prison? Really, Ryan? What would I be doing in a Turkish prison?"

"That was for illustrative purposes only, but you know what I mean. If you need me, I'll be there."

That answer seemed to satisfy her. "And I would do the same."

"So tomorrow...just act like you normally would. Don't avoid me because I won't be avoiding you. We have another seven days of shooting left. Let's just enjoy it and have fun."

She nodded and yawned. "I can do that. It will be nice getting back to work. This was a nice little vacation but I hate being stuck in the house this much. It will be good to get outside."

It would be good to get back to work. There wasn't much left to do on the picture and then he would have fulfilled his promise to Stan. He could then get back to his regularly scheduled projects. His career, which for all intents and purposes was his entire life.

But there was a big part of him that wouldn't mind staying here with Sierra for a while longer. A few days. Maybe a week.

———

The next day was easier than Sierra had imagined. Ryan was busy trying to catch up from the time they'd lost because of the storm so it wasn't like they had the chance to hang out and chat. Any free time that he may have had was sucked up by Angela, the other actress planting her ass in Ryan's trailer and not moving it unless she had a scene to do.

Feeling jealous was stupid. Ryan had made it clear how he felt about Angela but that didn't soothe Sierra even a little bit. The woman was making a fool of herself, that was for sure, but very few people seemed to be aware of it. Most of them thought that he was enjoying Angela's atten-tion. In fact, she overheard several people at lunch discussing "their affair" and wondering how quickly it would burn itself out.

If they only knew.

Sierra wasn't anxious to announce that she'd slept with Ryan but perversely she didn't want others to think he was sleeping with anyone else either.

I'm an idiot.

After grabbing a quick lunch, Sierra retreated to her own trailer for some peace and quiet. She tried to read but gave up after only a few pages. There was only one remedy for this mood. Billie.

Her sister answered on the second ring.

"Hey, how's the weather? Are you still all iced in?"

"It's fifty-two degrees today. It's like the ice never happened. I think spring has sprung."

"That's great. When will you be home? Are you almost done there?"

Sierra relaxed back in the soft chair, her tension beginning to melt. There was something about talking with family that did it for her. She could trust Billie with anything.

"That's a good question. The ice storm put us behind but Ryan's been working all day to juggle the schedule to finish on time. I assume that means some late nights and early mornings."

"It always does." Billie made a few sympathetic sounds before going silent for a moment. "So...how did it go?"

Sierra knew exactly what her sister was referring to but for some reason she wasn't feeling forthcoming about the details.

"It went fine. All good."

"Fine?" There was doubt in Billie's tone. "Just...fine? Oh honey, I'm so sorry."

Her sister thought that the sex had been bad or that Ryan had turned her down.

"It's not like what you're thinking. Really. It was good. Ryan's a great guy and we had a lot of fun. It's just..."

She didn't quite know how to describe what she was feeling.

"An inconsiderate lover?" Billie guessed. "A jerk? Did he not want to wear a condom? Men can be so selfish."

No one knew that better than Sierra, so it was funny that her sister was telling her that.

"Nothing like that," she assured Billie. "Seriously, he's a great guy. It's just so weird, I guess. We're back on the set today and no one knows what we did for the last two days. It's just surreal. I know it happened. I didn't dream it, but we agreed it would be over when we came back to the set. We're nice and friendly to one another but I can't help but remember that he saw me naked about twelve hours ago."

There was quiet on the other end of the phone and for a moment Sierra thought she'd lost the call. But as usual, Billie was simply formulating her next question and it was a doozy.

"It sounds like you really like him. I know you two made a deal but maybe you could talk to him about keeping this thing going between you. Have you thought about that?"

For a brief moment this morning when Sierra had woken up alone in her bed, she had thought about it. However, reality was a bitch and she was immediately reminded of all the reasons it was a lousy idea, not the least of which was that she didn't think Ryan was looking for anything more than a fling. The last thing Sierra needed was any kind of relationship. She was supposed to be exploring life and getting bogged down in emotions wasn't on the list.

"We made a deal," Sierra said. "And I'm going to stick to it. Neither one of us is in a place in our lives to do more than what we had. It was lovely but I guess I'm having a hard time moving on. This is all new to me. Maybe I'm not the wild and free type."

Billie's laughter could be heard clearly through the phone. "You may not be but that's okay. You tried and you had a good time. Everybody was an adult and nobody got hurt. You can move on to the next item on your list."

That's exactly what Sierra would do. Always look forward, never back. The future was in front of her and Ryan Ward was in the rearview mirror.

CHAPTER
Seventeen

RYAN STEPPED out of the tiny shower in his trailer and grabbed a towel to dry himself off, warm steam wafting around him. Wrapping the small rectangle around his waist, he stepped out of the closet they called a bathroom and into the main area only to find Angela lounging on his bed. This wasn't going to end well.

Shit. What in the hell did she want?

She was becoming a bigger problem than he'd anticipated. Angela simply wouldn't take no for an answer. He'd told her multiple times in multiple ways that he wasn't interested but she kept coming back to hear it again. He was getting tired of it and her.

"What are you doing here? Shouldn't you be in wardrobe?"

The little bitch had been sifting through his private mail, but she looked up at him and smiled like she hadn't just violated his privacy a few times over in the last few minutes.

"I wanted to talk to you about that. I'm not sure my character would wear that outfit."

He had shit to do. Important stuff.

"I don't give a rat's ass," he growled, not bothering to temper his rising anger. He had a reputation for making grown men cry and it was well-deserved. He had all the patience in the world - for a long time - but eventually the well was going to run dry. "Wear whatever you want. Wear nothing. Just get out. I have real work to do."

Her gaze ran up and down his body, lingering on the towel he'd forgotten was his only garb. Turning his back to her, he shrugged into a terry cloth robe, tightening the belt around his waist.

"Ohhhh, is Ryan a shy boy?" Angela cooed in a high squeaky voice that reminded him of nails on a chalkboard. She probably thought it was sexy. She'd be wrong. "I wouldn't have imagined that you were modest. Not with your reputation."

He'd never minded his reputation with women but at this moment he kind of wished he was a monk.

"Get out."

She stood up and walked closer to him. This trailer was far too small. "Now Ryan, don't be that way. We can have so much fun."

"Jesus, woman. For the last time, I'm not interested. Go hit on one of the extras or that reporter that keeps trailing around after you. But I'm not on the menu. Got it?"

She didn't have a chance to answer. There was a knock on the door and Sierra's voice on the other side.

"Ryan? They said you wanted to see me."

A moment of blind panic hit him. What to do?

"Just a second."

He needed to dress. He needed to get Angela out of here. And he needed to do it all in two seconds without alerting Sierra.

This won't look good.

As unbright as Angela was on most occasions she must have seen that panic on Ryan's face because she began to smile. Before he realized what she was doing or could even stop her, she'd pranced over to the door and opened it.

Holy hell.

"Come on in. Ryan and I are pretty much finished. For now."

Ryan could only stand in the middle of the trailer appalled at the entire situation that had to look damning to Sierra. He'd told her there was nothing going on with Angela and she'd believed him but this...

She stepped in looking gorgeous, her long hair in a mass of curls courtesy of the hair department. Her lips were done up in some shiny gloss and the first thing he thought about was what that pretty mouth could do.

Easy there, tiger.

Her gaze darted from Angela to Ryan to Angela and then finally back to him. "You wanted to talk to me?"

There was doubt in her tone and her body language was tense. Time to try and fix this.

"I do," he said firmly. "Angela, you should be in wardrobe."

The little bitch had been watching the back and forth with a shrewd gaze. Maybe she wasn't quite as dumb as he'd thought because she was putting two and two together and coming up with the fact that there was *something* between Ryan and Sierra.

Angela opened the door again and stepped out. "Ta ta, lover."

This time Ryan locked the door behind her. No one would get in without his knowing it.

"That wasn't what it looked like."

"I don't know what you mean."

They both knew what he was talking about.

"She was here when I came out of the shower. I didn't invite her."

"Okay."

"I'm not interested in her."

"You told me that."

"Well, it's true."

"I believe you." Sierra glanced over her shoulder to the closed door. "I'm not sure the rest of the cast and crew believe you, but I do."

He was relieved. "Good. Because it's the truth."

"It's none of my business anyway. We're not a couple or anything. You're free to do whatever or whomever you want."

Ryan sure as hell was. Why wasn't he happier about it? Sierra was smiling as if she'd received a pony for her birthday.

"I just wanted to be clear."

"You are. As crystal." She raised her brows in question. "You wanted to see me?"

What? Right. He had asked to see her. He'd spent all fucking night working on the stupid schedule and he wanted to tell her about the changes himself. He could have just posted them but that's not how he handled his actors. Whether he'd slept with them or not.

Now that she was here, however, and looking so beautiful he was thinking that maybe the changes he'd made to the schedule needed to be changed back. There were a million reasons why they couldn't continue their relationship but damned if he could remember even one of them at this moment. He did vaguely recall that those reasons were important though, so he needed to keep a lid on his libido. His little head didn't make the decisions around here.

"It's about the schedule."

"You were going to work on it."

He nodded and grabbed his tablet from the counter. "I was up all night and I've decided to cut the shopping scene. It's really not needed and we have the rest of the makeover scene, which is written far better."

Sierra didn't have the ego he'd seen in so many he'd worked with. She'd take her scene being cut like the professional that she was. But he'd still wanted to tell her personally.

"Okay, I think that's a good call. The scene was a little redundant."

She'd taken the news as he'd expected. He wouldn't mind working with her again. She'd done a great job with her character Molly. Sierra had talent, although she didn't seem to know it.

"So I moved your last scene up to tomorrow."

Tilting her head, her brows pulled together. "You moved the scene?"

He nodded, perusing the color-coded schedule one

more time. "I did. This way you'll be all finished by end of day tomorrow. I'm not sure what travel arrangements you've made but if you need help changing them just let one of the production assistants know and we'll help you. They can be available to give you a ride to the airport if you need it. Of course, you're welcome to stay in town and attend the wrap party. It's up to you."

He didn't want to look up and see her face but he did it anyway. Her cheeks were pink and her arms were crossed in front of her chest protectively. Shit, she'd taken it the wrong way. This was why he'd wanted to give her the news. Privately.

"This isn't what you're thinking, Sierra. I had to make changes to the schedule. You're only leaving three days early."

And I argued with myself for an hour at two in the morning before finally relenting and making the change.

"It's just a surprise, that's all. Actually, I'm anxious to get back home where it's warm."

He couldn't seem to stop explaining even though he had nothing to feel guilty for. This was business, and they were over. They'd agreed on that.

"This has nothing to do with us or what happened between us. This is how I can bring the movie in on time."

"It's fine, Ryan. There's little difference in tomorrow or a few days later. I do appreciate you letting me know. Is there anything else?"

He wanted to yes, that there was more but he wasn't sure what it was. He didn't want to see her go but their parting was inevitable. In the wee hours of the morning, he'd finally come to that conclusion. They had a great couple of days but that time was over. He had work to concentrate on and so did she. He really liked Sierra Oliver and if he'd been in a different place in his life...or a different person altogether...this scene might have a different ending.

"No, there's nothing else."

She murmured a thank you and turned on her heel and walked out of his trailer. For a brief moment he wanted to call to her, bring her back but that would have been a mistake.

They'd made an agreement. A fling and then go their separate ways. It was only coming three days earlier than planned. It didn't change the fact that there was no future between them.

With any other woman he would have been relieved that she was going home sooner rather than later. It just showed that Sierra wasn't just any woman. The man that she ended up with would be a lucky bastard.

It just wouldn't be Ryan.

————

Numb, Sierra walked back to the trailer she shared, grateful that she had it to herself. She wasn't sure what all she was feeling - or not feeling - and she wanted to sort it out alone. She'd purposely not allowed emotion to show on her face as she'd left Ryan's trailer. A movie set was a viper pit of gossip and she didn't want stories about her to begin making the rounds, although they wouldn't do it for long. The movie was scheduled to end production in a week.

For her...tomorrow. And she wouldn't be hanging around for the wrap party, either. She'd change her flight and get the heck out of town the minute Ryan said *cut*.

Now behind closed doors, she evaluated her reaction to the news critically. It was a little trick she'd learned in therapy to get in touch with her feelings.

Anger? There was a touch of that, but at least he'd had the nerve to tell her the change to her face. He could have just posted the new schedule and then avoided her for the next twenty-four to thirty-six hours.

Betrayal? Not really. He hadn't done anything but his job. The whole movie budget was a mess and he had to do something.

Sadness? This one. Right here. Sierra was sad that she was leaving him. She liked Ryan an awful lot and he didn't realize it but he'd gone a long way to restore her faith in men. Of course, Tyler and his friends had been the first to do that but Ryan had helped. She'd never had a sexual relationship with a man she was already *friends* with. She would miss it and him. The sex too, if she was brutally honest with herself.

I don't think I'm the fling type.

She hadn't expected to become this attached emotionally to Ryan. She'd spent the last eighteen months being detached from so much in life, it had been a shock to get close to him. She'd learned a long time ago not to get attached to people and things, but that lesson was becoming a distant memory. Her therapist, and Billie, would be thrilled.

Turning sad upside down, she needed to concentrate on what was good. She'd broken through a huge barrier with Ryan. She'd slept with a man again. She'd learned that sex could be as wonderful as she'd heard. She'd had a quick affair with a handsome man. This wasn't anything to be upset about.

More resolute after sorting out her feelings, Sierra reached for her phone to make the changes to her itinerary. It was time to go home. In a few months Ryan would be a lovely memory, a man she'd smile about whenever she heard his name or watched one of his movies.

Ryan Ward was many things. He was a great director, a wonderful lover, and a terrible camper. He didn't know shit about surviving an ice storm. He was a good man. But he wasn't her future.

CHAPTER
Eighteen

THE WAVES of the bluer than blue Caribbean lapped against the soft sand warmed by the sun. Sierra stretched out her legs and wriggled her painted toes before taking another sip of her fruity rum drink. The smell of sea, salt, and suntan lotion permeated the air and she took a deep breath, filling her lungs with the scent. It never ceased to make her happy and serene.

This was paradise.

Tyler and Billie had rented a luxurious home on the island of St. Thomas and that was why Sierra was sitting on the beach next to her sister under an umbrella, drinking a tasty libation. They'd gone swimming and sunbathing earlier and now they were relaxing in the shade, listening to the waves and the seagulls, and chatting about their plans when it was time to leave.

Sierra glanced over her shoulder at the house. "Where is Tyler? I haven't seen him in awhile."

"He went for a run. He has to stay in decent shape for this new movie."

"But he gets to keep his shirt on this time."

It was important to Tyler that his whole career not be based on his abs. He was excited about working with his close friends again. This wasn't a *Thunder* movie but a much more cerebral and suspenseful psychological thriller. Paige and Nate had penned the script and Max was even playing a bad guy, much to his glee. Nate, Tyler, and Sam were the men in white hats.

"He does and he's tickled to death about it." Billie tapped her fingers against the wooden table between their lounge chairs. "I have something to tell you about the movie."

Sierra's sister had been acting strangely these last few days. Actually, she'd begun wondering if Billie might be pregnant.

"Oh? What about it? Are you going to be in it?"

That would explain the strange behavior. Sierra would be left alone in Los Angeles while Billie and Tyler were on location. She'd be fine but her sister worried too much.

"In it? No." Billie shook her head and then sucked in a breath. "There's no other way to do this but to just say it."

Whoa. What was going on here? This didn't sound like a happy announcement like a baby.

"So spit it out."

"The director backed out of the movie at the last minute and now Ryan Ward is going to direct."

Billie's words hung in the air between them like a flashing neon sign in a bar window. Too bright to be ignored and twice as annoying.

Ryan Ward. Sierra hadn't heard that name in months. Of course, she'd gone out of her way not to, deliberately avoiding any gossip sites. She didn't want to see the latest actress he was bedding currently.

"Ryan to the rescue again," she finally replied, careful to keep her voice even. No one needed to know how often she thought about him. "If he's not careful he's going to get a reputation as a hero."

"We were lucky to get him." The words rushed out of Billie's mouth, all running together. "The movie he was working on lost its financing so he had a hole in his schedule."

Ryan Ward. Sierra was still trying to wrap her mind around it. Not that it mattered. She wasn't in the movie so she wouldn't see him.

"That's...great. He's a good director."

Billie was sneaking sideways glances at Sierra. They'd always been able to practically read each other's minds. It appeared that today was no exception.

"Are you okay with this?"

Sierra took another sip of her cool drink, the rum sliding down her tight throat. It hadn't been that way before she'd heard his name. "Does it matter? I won't see him or anything. I'm not in the movie."

"You could see him if you wanted to. I'm going to visit Tyler on location. You could come with me."

Her sister was only trying to help, but that would only make it worse.

"Not one good thing could come from that. Besides, you're assuming that he'd want to see me. I'm sure he's moved on by now. He probably has some beautiful actress on his arm. It's better if I stay away."

Billie sighed and moved restlessly in her chair. "This is all my fault. If I hadn't encouraged you to have a fling with him none of this would have happened. I'm so sorry, sis."

"It wasn't your fault. I was attracted to him and I slept with him. You didn't push me into bed with him. I'm a grown woman. I made my own decision."

"And now you regret it. He broke your heart."

Ah, if only it were that simple. Then she could just hate his guts and blame it all on him. Except nothing in life was that black and white.

"He didn't break my heart," Sierra replied, exasperated with her sibling. She was making this far more dramatic than it really was. "I just liked him much more than he liked me. I've come to the conclusion that I would have liked to continue the relationship to see where it might go."

Billie made a sour face. "He's not good enough for you."

Sierra giggled at her sister's dramatic antics. Always the actress. "He's not a bad person. He just wanted a brief thing. That's what I thought I wanted, too. It's not his fault that I changed my mind. Heck, when I left I thought it was for the best. And I don't regret sleeping with him. I'm glad I did it."

Thinking about him these last four months had made her feel more alive than she had in a long time. Missing him was an actual, real emotion that people felt every day. She'd shut so much of that down in pure self-preservation, but it wasn't healthy in the long term. Life hurt sometimes and it wasn't always going to be perfect sunshine and rainbows.

"I'm still sorry. I still feel like it's my fault."

Sierra set her drink down on the table. "You need to get over it."

"You need to get under it. I mean, get under another man."

Her eyes going wide, Sierra speared her sister with a look that would have quelled a lesser woman. "Excuse me, what did you say?"

Billie smiled. "The best way to get over a man is to get under a new one. That's a popular saying."

"So? There are lots of popular sayings. Early to bed and early to rise. If you can't stand the heat get out of the kitchen."

"Are you questioning the wisdom of Ben Franklin and Harry Truman?" Billie asked, sputtering with laughter. "Seriously, it's not the worst idea in the world. A new guy to get your mind off of the old one. Tyler has lots of handsome friends."

"Almost all of whom are actors. I don't want to date an actor. But thank you. Do I really seem that unhappy? I'm not."

Billie scrutinized her sister for a long minute. "You don't seem unhappy. You seem...subdued. Like you're thinking all the time. Do you think about him a lot?"

It wasn't the quantity that was the problem, it was the quality.

"Surprisingly, not that often. Just every now and then when something reminds me of him. I can go days and not think about him."

She had gone days. At least once, maybe twice.

"What reminds you?"

A smile curved Sierra's lips as she remembered back. "Toasted marshmallows. The cold. A roaring fire. Spaghetti with tomato sauce. Chocolate chip cookies. Robert DeNiro."

"Uh...DeNiro?"

"DeNiro."

Billie leaned forward, her gaze darting around them before settling on Sierra. "Sis, do you become aroused watching *Raging Bull*?"

It was too much. Sierra couldn't stop the laughter that bubbled up at Billie's silly question. She was also sure that it was intentional on her sister's part.

"It's no shame," Billie said with a somber expression. "We can get you help."

Hold her aching ribs, Sierra dashed at the tears leaking from her eyes. "You are such a goof ball. No, I do not need help."

"The first step—"

"For heaven's sake, stop it," Sierra scolded. "It was a few days out of my life. I liked him and I still do. Heck, if the relationship had gone on we probably would have crashed and burned by week six. I think it's just that now I'll never know. That's what is bugging me."

It was a point of which Sierra had constantly reminded herself. Even if they had tried to date, they wouldn't have made it. Hollywood, careers, and a man that didn't do commitment weren't conducive to relationship bliss. It wouldn't have worked.

Billie's expression turned serious and a little sad. "Did you love him?"

Sierra had stayed awake more nights than she could count thinking about that very question.

"I think that I did in a small way," she answered with a smile. "And I don't regret what I felt. I think that I *could* have fallen in real love with him if we'd had enough time."

Time. It had simply never been on their side.

But she had many years ahead of her and she couldn't spend them thinking about Ryan.

CHAPTER
Nineteen

IT WAS time for the table reading of the script and the entire cast was assembled on the soundstage. Tables had been set up in a circle so they were all facing each other. Ryan twisted open the top of a bottle of water and watched as the main actors rolled in, laughing and talking like the old friends they were. This movie was going to be perhaps the easiest job he'd ever done.

The cast was filled with consummate professionals who knew when to take direction and also when to tell Ryan to blow it out of his ass. Sam Collins especially took no shit from anyone and Tyler Gaylord had a reputation for giving no fucks. The script was a dream and they were all excited and ready to work. Hell, even the budget and schedule were reasonable. All in all, Ryan should be having the time of his life.

I shouldn't have taken this job.

He'd been lured in by the amazing casting and the exotic locales. A few more countries ticked off of his bucket list, plus he'd always wanted to work with Nate Mason, Maxwell Hayes, Tyler Gaylord, and Sam Collins. He'd be lying, though, if he didn't admit - at least to himself - that he'd almost turned the movie down. Where Tyler Gaylord was, there was a chance of Sierra being there as well.

After almost five months since he'd seen her, he was still confused as hell. No one in his entire life had stuck in his head this long. It was as if she'd taken up residence in a part of his brain and she strolled out every now and then just to remind him that she was still around. He thought of her at the most inopportune moments. Just the other night he'd had a date and she'd talked about her brother taking his kids camping and toasting marshmallows.

Suddenly he'd been back in Sierra's living room, sitting in front of that warm fire and feeding her marshmallows. Her pink tongue sliding across those full lips to get every last drop. He'd gone hard at the mere memory.

The date hadn't gone anywhere, either. In fact, none of them had lately. He'd put it down to being so busy he'd barely slept but the fact was he just wasn't interested in other women. He constantly compared them to Sierra and they all came up short.

Christ, it was bad. He needed a brain purge but he had a sneaky feeling that she'd still have a piece of his heart.

Somewhere around the end of month two he'd admitted that he might have fallen a little in love with her. More like a crush than a full blown "let's spend the rest of our lives together" kind of thing. She'd been so different than the women he'd dated in the past and he'd almost thrown himself on the trunk of the car that drove her away from the set that last day. He'd told himself that it was for the best, that they didn't have any sort of future.

He still believed it. He'd thought about what might have happened if he'd asked her to stick around, maybe jet off with him to some vacation spot where they could have spent their days on the beach and their nights making love. It would have been heaven, but then reality would eventually intrude and he'd have to fly off somewhere and make a movie. The separation would weigh on their relationship and eventually one of them would end it. No, they'd been right to leave it the way they did. Now they only had good memories.

The actors had settled into their chairs and were staring at him expectantly. Shit, he'd been gone again. Back to Sierra's dark little condo during the storm. He needed to be sure to keep too busy to allow that to happen often.

"Welcome," he said, flipping open his script. All business, dammit. "I'll save the introductions for later during lunch. Let's get going on this table read. Any questions before we get started?"

If anyone wondered about his abrupt greeting they didn't say so aloud. Time to get to work.

———

Tyler had never seen a man avoid a topic as doggedly as Ryan Ward avoided asking or talking about Sierra. In the two weeks they'd been working together on this film, it would have been normal and natural for one or both of them to have brought up Ryan's work with Sierra. The one time Tyler had brought it up?

Ward had shut down the conversation and immediately changed the subject. Even his expression had changed to a little bit nervous and panicked. Tyler had felt so sorry for the poor bastard that he'd respected the man's wishes, although there was a part of him that wanted to pull the director aside and tell him that he was fighting a futile battle.

Tyler ought to know. He'd fallen for one twin and he wasn't ever getting out. Not that he wanted to. He didn't. He'd never been happier in his life but a confirmed bachelor like Ryan Ward had to be sweating bullets.

There was another part of Tyler that also wanted to punch Ward in the face and hope it would knock some sense into him. Sierra was definitely pining for the man and Billie couldn't seem to convince her sister to move on. These two people just might have fallen in love with one another. Tyler didn't blame Sierra for their separation. The young woman didn't know shit about relationships, love, sex, or men. But Ryan Ward? He fucking knew better, or at least he should.

That one thought had been festering away inside of Tyler for two whole damn weeks.

That's why when Ward was working with them to block out a fight scene, Tyler took the opportunity to take a swing at the other man. To an innocent bystander it would look like an accident but Tyler wanted to make sure that Ryan knew exactly why he'd been clocked in the jaw. As the director staggered back, Tyler leaped forward to catch him before he hit the wall behind him, but he also took the opportunity to whisper in Ward's ear.

"That was for Sierra, you son of a bitch."

Stalking off the set, Tyler headed for his trailer with Sam Collins on his heels. He ignored the older actor but Sam just reached out and grabbed Tyler's arm, whipping him around.

"I'm sure he deserved it but I still wonder why you just punched our director."

"It was an accident."

Sam grinned and took a step back. "You made it look that way but I've seen too many movie fights to believe that. What's going on?"

Tyler wasn't sure that Sierra wanted her business spread all over but this was Sam. The story wouldn't go any further. This man could keep a secret.

"He worked with Sierra about four months ago. They had a fling."

Sam and Sierra were good friends and he'd given her a big break in movies. He was also incredibly protective. It might not have been a good idea to tell him after all. Sam's face clouded over and he looked pissed the hell off.

"What did you say?"

Tyler sighed and glanced over his shoulder, ensuring they wouldn't be overheard.

"They had a little on-set fling. They both agreed it would be casual but I guess Sierra kind of fell for the asshole."

Sam's brows pinched together and his lips flattened into a straight line. "Then we should all take a swing at him. I'll get Nate and Max."

Tyler shook his head. "I shouldn't have done it. They made a deal. Ward didn't do anything wrong. Not really. I just hate seeing Sierra so sad. I doubt he's worth it."

Sam appeared to agree. "I don't know anyone who is good enough for Sierra. Or Billie, for that matter. We're all watching you, by the way. Make that woman cry and we'll beat your ass."

"Charming. With friends like you..."

Sam just laughed. "Fuck you, right? I get it. Let's face it. All of us overachieved in the love department. None of us are good enough for our wives. So what are we going to do about Sierra and Ward? Do you think he still has feelings for her?"

"You are such a matchmaker," Tyler taunted his friend. "How the hell would I know? Do you think he dreamily doodles Sierra's name in a pink notebook with unicorn stickers?"

"I hope not," Sam snorted. "Seriously, maybe he thinks she wanted to end things, and she thinks he wanted to end things, but they're both wrong. Now they're alone and miserable. Jesus, I think I just described a romantic comedy."

"You did and it's already been made about a zillion times."

The sound of footsteps behind Tyler captured his attention. He didn't even have to turn around to know who it was. He and Ryan were about to have a talk. Man to man.

CHAPTER
Twenty

PHONE TO EAR, Billie stepped out onto the patio and closed the French doors behind her just in case Sierra was anywhere in the vicinity. She didn't want her sister listening in on this conversation.

"You punched him? Why on earth did you do that? He didn't do anything wrong."

"Sierra's unhappy and he's the reason."

Men and their testosterone. They had a great deal to answer for in this crazy world.

"I wouldn't say she's unhappy. She's a little melancholy. She fell for him. So what did he do after you punched him? Did he hit you back?"

Her husband chuckled as if it was all so hilarious. "He wanted to. After he finished blocking the scene he came after me and demanded to know what I was talking about."

"Wait...talking about?"

There was a small pause before Tyler answered. "I

might have whispered in his ear that the punch was for Sierra."

Christ on a unicycle. These actors were so dramatic and over the top.

"Tyler Gaylord, what were you thinking? Does Ryan Ward now think that Sierra wanted his lights punched out? Because she doesn't."

"He knows that now," Tyler admitted, chagrin in his tone. "I just told him that I didn't appreciate how he dealt with Sierra. She's really innocent and naive."

No, not really. In a way, she was far wiser than all of them put together after what she'd been through. Did she need to learn how to date like a normal person? Yes. Did that mean she was innocent? Sadly, no. That had been stripped away from her years ago.

"If I tell her you did this, she's going to kick you in your balls. What was his response?"

"He said that he really liked her but that he knew he couldn't give her the kind of relationship she deserved, what with his work all over the globe. He said that if he hurt her he didn't mean to. He kind of, in a roundabout way, admitted that he missed her, too."

Which was all fine and dandy but Ryan Ward hadn't done a thing to get Sierra back into his life. If he wanted her, he needed to make a move. Same with Sierra. Love and happily ever after didn't just magically appear. If they wanted it, they had to earn it. They had to make it happen.

"So have you two kissed and made up? You still have several weeks of shooting left."

"We're fine. I told him he could take a free swing at me

but he declined. We went out and had some beers. I picked up the check. It's all good, babe."

Another thing Billie would never understand about men. They could be beating the shit about of each other one minute and buddies the next.

"Try not to beat anyone else up, okay?"

"I'll try not to but Nate pulled another one of his famous practical jokes yesterday. Payback is imminent."

"I don't even want to know what you're going to do. Leave me out of it."

Tyler didn't reply for so long that she almost thought the call had been dropped.

"So we're not going to do anything? Not a thing?"

Billie sighed and sat down on one of the patio chairs. It was another sunny day in California. "Nothing. If they love each other, they're going to have to figure it out themselves. I'm not going to insert myself into the middle of their relationship. They're adults."

"If Ryan is anything like I was, he's clueless when it comes to women and love."

"Yes, but you figured it out."

"He might not be as smart as I am."

Laughing, Billie propped her feet up on another chair. "We're going to have to take that chance. I love my sister but I've learned that she doesn't want us interfering in every aspect of her life. She likes to be independent; Tyler, and you know that. She needs to deal with this on her own."

"I know." There was sadness in Tyler's voice but also acceptance. "I just worry about her."

Billie couldn't have picked a better husband.

"And I love you for that. I know that you and all of your friends do but she's getting stronger and more mentally healthy every single day. It's time to give her wings. We've already given her roots."

"When did you get so wise?"

"Pay attention. I've always been that way. Now get back to work."

More than anything Billie wanted Sierra to have the love and happiness that she had with Tyler, but she couldn't hand it to her on a silver platter. If Sierra still wanted Ryan, she needed to go for it.

On her own.

Ryan should have been sleeping, but instead he was sitting up in bed staring at a tabloid photo of Sierra and her sister Billie shopping. They were carrying several shopping bags and had big smiles on their faces, laughing at some joke that one of them had told.

Sierra looked good.

She was always beautiful but her entire face was lit up with happiness. She didn't appear to be missing him in the least, which was good. Right? They'd parted for all of the right reasons and neither one of them needed an unre-quited love.

He had wonderful memories of their time together, but they didn't have a future. It was sad but that's just the way it was.

Sierra padded into the main house on bare feet, hair still damp from her shower. She'd worked out until she was ready to collapse and now all she wanted was some dinner and then bed. The delicious smells emanating from the kitchen made her stomach growl insistently.

"Come in," Billie called to Sierra, waving a big wooden spoon in the air. "I'm making spaghetti. It's just what you need after a hard workout."

Probably not, although Sierra still had a hard time keeping the pounds on. Weight training had helped fill out her figure and make her look less waif-like but it had also fired up her metabolism. Now she needed to eat even more calories.

The smell of tomatoes and garlic, the sight of pasta bubbling away took Sierra directly back to the ice storm and Ryan. It had been a simple meal but somehow it had tasted better than anything she'd had to eat in a long time.

"You're thinking about him again, aren't you? Shit, I should have made tacos."

Automatically, her head shook in denial even though Billie wouldn't buy it for a second.

"I'm not."

"You are."

She sighed, leaning over the pot and breathing in the aroma. "Maybe I am. It's no big deal."

"You could call him. Or email him. If you don't have the number, we can get it from Tyler. Or you could come with me next week when I visit the set."

Billie was going to spend a few weeks with Tyler while the cast and crew were on location in Las Vegas. It sounded like a horrifying idea to go along.

"You know I can't."

"You can't, or you won't?"

"It's the same thing."

"It's not the same at all and you know it." Billie placed the spoon down on a saucer. "You know, he might be thrilled to see you."

"Or not."

"You're not willing to take the chance?"

There was a part of her that wanted to. But...

"He watched me leave," Sierra finally said, her voice soft. "He let me leave, Billie. Hell, he made it so that I left *early*. I'm just afraid that if I take the chance that I'll end up really hurt this time."

"You want him to make the first move. I don't blame you. You want a grand gesture."

Billie didn't understand. This wasn't a movie.

"I don't need a big gesture." Sierra shook her head sadly. "I just want a sign. One little sign. Then I'll make the next move."

———

Location shooting was always a hassle unless they were out in the middle of nowhere, but even then there were challenges such as electricity. The streets of Las Vegas were proving to be a complete nightmare. The crowds and traffic were worse than he'd remembered from his last trip there - a bachelor party for a buddy. In complete frustration, Ryan had had the security guards push the barriers back another ten feet. People were taking flash photography with their phones and ruining his shot. He was about ready to throw out the next person that did it.

The crew was changing the lighting so everyone had a ten-minute break. Ryan took a long drink from his water bottle but then almost choked on its contents. Coughing and sputtering, he did a double-take, blinking his eyes as if he was seeing a mirage in the surrounding desert.

Was that...Sierra?

She was standing next to Max and Nate, her back to Ryan. He'd been afraid to ask Tyler if she might accompany Billie out here and it looked like she just might have. His heart hammered against his ribs and his mouth went cotton dry. *Sierra.* It was as if his constant thinking about her had made her manifest here just for him. He hadn't been able to shake her no matter what he did. She haunted his dreams at night - when he managed to sleep - and practically every waking moment. He'd been arguing with himself about the futility of calling her, maybe asking Tyler for her phone number, but he hadn't yet worked up the courage.

Just then Tyler joined the little group and Sierra whirled around and threw herself into his arms. Wait–

It was Billie.

From the back he'd mistaken her for Sierra but from the front there was no denying who it was. His heart fell to his feet and the breath seemed to leak from his body, leaving him slumped against his chair. Tired and worn out.

I surrender. I can't go on like this.

So? What are you going to do about it?

I don't know, but I'm clearly losing my mind.

If Sierra had been here, there was no doubt as to what he'd do.

Make a complete and utter fool of himself.

Surely by now Sierra had moved on even if he hadn't. She'd looked truly happy in that tabloid photo. She wasn't missing him and he needed to get his head on straight. No more mooning over a woman. And she was just a woman. He'd had many in the past and there would be more in the future. She was only one of them.

Sierra was the past and it was time to put her there.

CHAPTER
Twenty~One

SIERRA TAPPED her foot impatiently and peered out of the darkened windows of the limousine. They were waiting in a long car line to walk the red carpet at the first awards ceremony of the year and she could hear the roar of the crowds from inside the vehicle.

"You aren't nervous, are you?" Tyler asked, lounging back against the soft leather seats. "You've done this before."

She had and normally this wouldn't be a big deal. Walk. Smile. Pose. Smile. Walk some more. Tonight, however, was different.

Tonight *he* would be here.

"I'm fine. Just tired."

This would be the first time Sierra had seen Ryan in months. She'd heard about him from Tyler but she hadn't seen him. He was presenting an award so unless she hid in the bathroom at that exact moment she wasn't going to be able to miss him.

"Thanks for coming tonight. I hate going to these events alone."

Sierra smiled, the first of many tonight. She'd be doing it until her face hurt.

"It's no problem. I just hope Billie takes the doctor's advice and stays off of that ankle."

Sierra's sister was training for a new role and had hurt herself, spraining her ankle. The doctor had assured them it wasn't serious but she needed to stay off of it for a few days. That meant she couldn't attend the awards ceremony tonight.

Enter Sierra. They were both about the same size so she was even able to wear the new dress that Billie had chosen for the event. Tyler had joked that the two resembled each other so much that no one might even know that he had a different sister on his arm. Sierra would be fine with that. She still wasn't used to all of the attention and fuss. She didn't mind it but she simply didn't understand it. People asked for her autograph but she really hadn't done anything that earth shattering. Not like Tyler and Billie. Or Ryan.

Tyler flashed his Hollywood smile as the limo took its turn pulling up to the red carpet.

"Are you ready to do this? Flash those pearlies."

The flash of cameras was almost blinding and she could hear her name, Billie's name, and Tyler's name all being screamed by the crowd of onlookers. It appeared that some knew who she was and others assumed that her sister was standing next to Tyler.

Allowing Tyler to take control, he led her to the first backdrop where they'd have their picture taken by every photojournalist in Hollywood. Tyler stayed close but not too close, careful not to touch her as they posed. The gossips in this town were the worst and tabloids were already speculating just how long Billie and Tyler would last. Sierra being at his side was only going to make it worse. They didn't need to fuel the fire with a public display of brother-sister affection.

Sierra kept her gaze facing forward but it wasn't easy. She wanted to look around and see if he was there. Was he standing off to the side? Had he seen her yet? If they ran into each other, what would she say?

You've ruined me for other men, asshole.

I hate your guts but I think I might also be in love with you.

You make me crazy. I want to knee you in the jewels.

"Relax," Tyler said out of the corner of his mouth, still smiling as the flashbulbs popped. "You're stretched tighter than a bow. And I swear if you say you're fine one more time, my head is going to pop off and fly into the air. That will definitely make the news tonight."

"I am a little nervous," she admitted, but not the reason why. Let him think it was the crowds.

"I don't see him anywhere. He may have already arrived. We ran kind of late."

Her head jerked and she looked up at him, open-mouthed. "I wasn't–"

Tyler laughed and nudged her so that she was facing the cameras again. "You were but it's okay. I'll punch him again if you want me to."

Again?

"When did you punch him the first time?"

Clearing his throat, Tyler moved them along the

gauntlet and somehow managed to slip past the woman from the entertainment network interviewing anyone who was somebody. Tyler was absolutely a somebody.

"Does it really matter? The important thing is you're fine."

They ducked into the venue and Tyler's publicist, who had been cooling his heels while they walked the carpet, was frantically waving to them. They needed to take their seats. "Tyler Gaylord, you better start talking."

"It's not what you think."

"Did you punch him?"

"Yes."

"Then it's exactly what I think."

———

Ryan was presenting the award for Best Director and it had all been going great. He'd practiced pronouncing all of the nominees' names over and over until they came out smooth as silk. Even the really difficult ones.

It was a good night. The weather had cooperated, his tux fit well, and he hadn't been asked any stupid questions by interviewers. All in all, it was a banner evening and only getting better. He'd present this award, spend a little time at the after party, and then head back to his home in Malibu. Due to the availability of his leading man, the start date for Ryan's next picture had been pushed back for two months. For the first time in years he was at loose ends for longer than a week. He was contemplating taking some time and traveling, or he might sit at home and work on that script he'd been messing with for years.

I could do both.

So he'd been on a roll, announcing the nominees and having a grand old time when his gaze landed on *her.*

She was sitting next to Tyler in the second row and looking up at Ryan.

It was like being punched in the gut and then just when you get your breath back, having another land on your jaw. Right about where Tyler had punched him.

Dammit, she wasn't supposed to look this beautiful. He'd convinced himself that it was only his imagination that had made her so gorgeous. The reality was far different, he'd told himself. Sierra Oliver was actually rather ordinary.

That theory had been blown out of the water.

What is she doing here with Tyler? How did I not know she was attending?

Sucking in a breath, he managed to not stutter as he announced the winner. Gratefully stepping back when the man reached the podium to give his acceptance speech, Ryan had a brief moment to study Sierra from a distance without any attention on him. Did she know he was going to be here? Was that why she came? Or did she attend in spite of it?

Too many questions and no answers.

One more question rolled around his befuddled brain. Would she be at the after party?

Because if she was...he wanted - no, needed - to talk to her. This was insane. He was insane. But he couldn't deny what he was feeling inside any longer. Not when he was looking at her and he wanted to see her face all the time.

He had two months before his next movie started. That

was enough to give a relationship a decent start. After that, they could play it by ear. He didn't have to work all the time, and they might be able to work together, too. It could happen.

All he needed was a second chance.

CHAPTER
Twenty~Two

SIERRA CHECKED the time on her cell phone. She and Tyler had agreed they would stay an hour and then go home. It would be just long enough to shake some hands and be seen. They were both anxious to get home and check on Billie, who had hopefully followed the doctor's instructions.

One hour. One drink.

She'd mingled and smiled, congratulating winners and consoling the losers. This was a competitive town and even when an actor didn't have a snowball's chance in hell in winning there was always that small hope that they might pull it out. Luckily there was enough food and free booze to soothe a million bruised egos.

The party was in full swing, with music, dancing, and loud laughter. Tyler had been cornered by the entertainment reporter they'd managed to duck earlier. Not wanting the same for herself, Sierra slipped out of the side entrance to the little terrace area where the caterer had set up a staging area. She received a few strange looks from the waiters and waitresses but no one told her she couldn't be out there.

Leaning against the wrought iron fence, she sipped at her martini and relaxed. It was a lovely night, the breeze warm. It looked like she wasn't going to run into Ryan tonight, which was probably a blessing. It had been hard enough to see him up on stage. He looked so handsome and sexy in his tuxedo, although she would forever prefer him in jeans and a sweatshirt. If he'd walked out dressed like that she might have run up on stage and tackled him. Thank goodness for Armani.

"Sierra."

Sucking in an audible breath, she froze, recognizing that voice easily. A deep, smooth baritone that she'd heard in her dreams over and over until she thought she'd go mad. Her fingers tightened on the martini glass and she had to force herself to turn around slowly, show no emotion. He didn't need to know how deeply this meeting affected her. He was probably just being polite and saying hello. He'd said they would be friends, right?

"Ryan." She was shocked her lips could form words. "Nice job tonight. I'm sorry you weren't nominated, too."

He walked closer and she caught a whiff of his body wash, spicy and citrus. There was also a hint of whiskey, too. "Thank you. I can't be nominated every year. That's unrealistic."

He rested his elbow on the fence, his body inches from her own. Too close. Far too close. From this distance she could reach out and touch him. That would be a mistake.

With a shaking hand, she placed her glass on the table next to her.

"I didn't expect to see you tonight. Where's your sister?"

I can do this. I can act like it's all fine.

"She sprained her ankle during a training session. Tyler didn't want to come alone."

"Her misfortune is my good luck."

Huh? Sierra shook her head in confusion. She didn't understand.

"I beg your pardon?"

He smiled then and reached out, placing his hand on top of hers. His flesh was warm and it stole the breath from her lungs, leaving her standing there baffled and about to faint from lack of oxygen.

"I said that I'm sorry she's hurt but I'm glad you came."

"Oh."

Sierra didn't know what to say to that. Her head hurt trying to make heads or tails out of Ryan's words. Frankly, if she didn't get away soon she was going to do something embarrassing like throw her body against his.

"I should go find Ty–"

His fingers tightened on hers and his smile fell. "Please don't. I need to talk to you."

She hesitated, wanting badly to flee but there had been something in his tone that made her stay.

"Please," he said again, his gaze searching her face for... What? She didn't know, but she was still having trouble breathing and her pulse had sped up far too fast. If she wasn't careful she'd faint. "Five minutes. After that, if you want to leave I won't try to stop you."

"Okay. What–What did you want to talk about?"

Her stomach tumbled in her abdomen. There was fear there but there was also the tiniest bit of hope. She was a fool to nurture it. He was only going to smash it into a thousand pieces, but she couldn't seem to extinguish the small flame inside of her that wished he felt the same way as she did.

"Us. I want to talk about us."

"There is no us," she replied quickly. "We made an agreement."

Baring his teeth, Ryan growled so loudly she jumped, along with a few of the waiters milling in the background. Heads whipped around and he cleared his throat, clearly embarrassed that he'd called attention to them. He dipped his head low so that only she could hear what he had to say.

"Fuck that agreement," he said through gritted teeth. "I fucking hate that agreement. I've been regretting it and I wish we'd never made it."

The twisting in her gut had turned into a thousand butterfly wings. She was glad she was holding onto the fence because her knees had turned into jelly.

Hold your horses, missy. Find out what he wants. Is it just a booty call?

"Really? Why?'

She congratulated herself on sounding so casual when in reality she was about to jump out of her skin.

He removed his hand from hers and scraped his fingers through his hair, clipped much shorter than the last time she'd seen him.

"I just kept telling myself that it wouldn't work. That

my career would get in the way and you'd lose patience with me. I told Tyler that and he seemed to get it."

"Tyler? You spoke to Tyler about me?"

Her sneaky brother-in-law had never said a word. Billie had to know as well.

Heads will roll.

"Right after he decked me. He said that you were missing me. Believe me, honey, that hit me right in the gut. I'd been missing you too, but I didn't think I could make a relationship work over the long haul. I thought I'd fail."

"I'm sorry he hit you. I just found out about that tonight." Something Billie had said to her a few months ago stuck in Sierra's mind. If she wanted something, she had to have the courage to go after it. Ryan had taken the first step tonight. She'd sworn that if he did, she'd take the second. "You say you've missed me but you thought you'd fail. How do you feel now?"

Holding her breath, she waited for his reply. It was all down to his next sentence. No pressure here.

"I want to take a chance with you, Sierra. If you'll take a chance on me." He held up his hands when she would have answered. "Listen to me. I'm stubborn and I get lost in my work. I'm ambitious and I'd be lying if I said that I'm not a workaholic. I'm a slob and I have no fucking clue what to do in an ice storm but..."

"But?" she prompted, tears burning the backs of her eyes. She had to blink to keep them from ruining her eye makeup.

"But damn, I've fallen in love with you. And if you just give me another chance, I want to prove that to you. I actually have the next two months off and I want to spend every minute with you if I can. Let's see if this relationship has legs. My life isn't the same without you."

All the things Sierra had fantasized about him saying and here he was...saying them. It was almost too good to be true. There was just one thing still bothering her.

"But you sent me away early..."

He shook his head, his hands sliding up her arms and resting on her bare shoulders, sending tingles down her spine.

"I changed the schedule because of the movie, not because of you. You have no idea how hard it was to watch you leave that day."

"I have an idea," she murmured, a warmth filling her heart. "You want a second chance? To try? What happens at the end of two months? Do we go our separate ways again?"

She couldn't do that. She knew herself too well now. Casual wasn't her style.

"Absolutely not." There was no equivocation in his tone. "We figure it out. Maybe make a movie together. I won't take every job that comes along. I'll travel with you now and then and hopefully you can travel with me. We'll work on that list of yours and mine, too. I want to make compromises for you, Sierra."

That was more powerful than any declaration of love because he'd never made compromises for anyone before.

"I want to make compromises for you, too. I love you, Ryan, and I don't say that lightly."

She hadn't intended to fall in love her first time out of the gate after her divorce but she wasn't sorry in the least.

Ryan Ward was a good man. One of the best. Her judgment hadn't let her down.

This time she did throw herself into his arms just as she'd imagined. Their kiss started slow and gentle before turning into something sizzling hot and filled with promise. They had a future. It wasn't going to be easy but they were both determined to make it work. No one knew better than Sierra that happily ever after was only stories. This was real life. But what a life she had to look forward to. Traveling, work, loving this man. It would be worth it.

So caught up in each other, they didn't see Tyler slip into the terrace to tell Sierra it was time to go home. They didn't see his grin of delight or watch him immediately text Billie, who told him to leave the two lovebirds alone.

They'd find their way home together.

I hope you enjoyed Ryan and Sierra's happily ever after!

Looking for your next read? Check out the steamy romantic comedy series from Olivia Jaymes – ManTrap.

Thank you for reading And the Winner is!

About the Author

Olivia Jaymes is a wife, mother, lover of sexy romance, and caffeine addict. She lives with her husband and son in central Florida and spends her days with handsome alpha males and spunky heroines.

Visit Olivia Jaymes at
www.OliviaJaymes.com